To :

BOLDLY GO

Enjoy

B P Hall

BARRY P HALL

Boldly Go

tellwell

Tellwell Talent
www.tellwell.ca

ISBN
978-0-2288-3414-4 (Paperback)

ACKNOWLEDGEMENTS

Thank you to Richard Lutz for all his help with this manuscript.

Thank you to the following people for the use of their names. All characteristics displayed in this book are fictitious. Only the names were used:

Alfred and Bonnie Black

Sue McGregor

Bruce Monfils

David Stead

Any similarities to their true nature are completely incidental.

CHAPTER 1

It had been a very wet, blustery spring. The weather was totally unpredictable but certainly wet. What was I, a fifty-eight-year-old retired country gentleman, doing wading around in the mud in rubber boots on a Friday morning? I guess I did have an excuse. It was to be the first day of horse racing this spring at Morrow Park Racetrack in Peterborough. My favourite gelding, Kingston Kenny, was getting older and he was scheduled to run later today in the fifth race. He no longer liked fast or hard tracks. Maybe his feet were sore, but he preferred soft or muddy going. I just didn't want him breaking a leg when it was too much for him to handle. The track officials were still trying to decide if the track was fit to race on today. My friend George had Joe Cool in the second race, while my other friend, Robert, had Sam's Friend in the sixth. Many owners did not like to race with the track like this, but in a week it could easily be dry and hard.

I saw Harry, the track manager, start to walk toward the clubhouse. I assumed he had made the decision whether to race or close up for the day. The weather today was just overcast, no rain in sight. It looked like a go for racing, so I started to the clubhouse to check with the brain trust. As I had guessed, the racing was a go for today, so I called our Peterborough trainer, John, to tell him the good news and ask him to send us a driver.

Being satisfied that our first racing day of the spring was going to happen, I headed to our favourite café to get a coffee and a bite to eat. George and Robert were both there ahead of me, anxious to know whether racing would be going ahead today. George, the joker in the group, was excited about the chances of his baby, Joe Cool. I had to admit he always ran better on an off track.

George had been a police officer in the city of Toronto before the war, and that experience—plus all the carnage he had witnessed on the job—had prompted him to retire when it was over and become a country gentleman, like myself.

Robert, the third member of our bunch, was by far the best pilot of all of us. He had flown Spitfires in the Battle of Britain and had been fighting overhead when his family was blown to bits during a German bombing raid. That had affected him badly, but I guess we were all three suffering from shell shock. We were all now pilots, with George the last to get his wings the year before. All three of us also had harness horses in training and were enthusiastic about the sport.

"How did the track look, Ron?" said Robert.

"Just a couple of inches of mud," I replied. "Good enough to run the races today. Kingston Kenny should like the going. It's good to have the racing at home again."

"Yeah, I'm tired of going all the way to Toronto," said George. "I like our home track better."

"We have a lot of good friends around here to chat with," I replied.

"From my point of view, it's the best entertainment around," said Robert.

"Changing the subject," I said, "I had a telephone call from an old friend last night. He was a theoretical physicist at the University of Toronto up until retired. We went through university together years ago and became good friends We lived together in the same room in the dorm then. I haven't seen him in years. He's asked us to come and visit him in Smith's Falls for a few days. When I asked what it was about, he wouldn't tell me, but he was very excited. You could say he was over the top. I've never known him to be so excited. Would you guys want to come with me?"

"Did you ask him if it was okay to bring two guests?" asked George.

"Of course," I replied. "Actually, he seemed delighted that there would be two more people."

"When do we go?" inquired Robert, always the practical one.

"He wanted us tomorrow, but I talked him into waiting until Monday," I said. "He didn't seem too pleased about waiting, but he always was an impatient person. Is that all right with you fellows?"

"Yes," they chorused, always eager to do something new.

"Let's get something for lunch then we can head for the track and some racing," said George.

John, our trainer, had sent Will to drive. I liked having Will; he was a good steadying hand on the reins. The best on an off track. The second race came up quick with George's Joe Cool running. Will took him out to the front from the start and he stayed there with no trouble at all. George was dancing, he had a winner. George loved winners.

John certainly seemed to have chosen the right horseshoes. Horseshoes were a tricky part of the racing scene. Joe Cool had raced the course without a slip, even with the mud. I could see horses out between the races that were slipping; they probably had regular shoes on. Hopefully, the owners or trainer could get them reshod before their races came up.

As George had a winner, he bought the between-races coffee. As he was getting our order, I saw a tall, distinguished-looking woman of about fifty talking to him and trying to give him a paper of some kind.

George appeared agitated. Finally, he said in a loud angry voice, "Leave me alone. I don't want any of your truck." Harry, the track manager, looked up from where he was sitting in the far corner, got up and started toward George and the woman. She started to move away, at which point Harry had a brief word with George and then went after the woman.

George brought the coffee over to the table.

"What was that all about?" Robert asked.

"Jehovah's Witness," said George. "I don't like that crowd; they have some very crazy ideas in my opinion."

"Don't let them spoil your day," I said. "They certainly work hard for their faith."

"Maybe so," said George, "but I don't agree with much of their doctrine."

"I was asked one time to be a Jehovah's Witness," I said, "but I had to turn them down. I hadn't even seen the accident."

The snort of laughter that came from George carried half a mouthful of coffee. Some even went up his nose. It took a few minutes to recover his aplomb and get himself cleaned up. When he was back to normal, he said, "That's a good one. I never heard that before."

"We had to do something to restore your good humour," I said. "The day has been good so far."

"That helped a little, but Harry just told me Joe Cool was claimed, so I won a race but lost my horse."

"That's racing for you." I laughed.

"Don't laugh so soon," said George. "Harry said there's a claim in for Robert's horse and your horse, as well. At least you have time to scratch them if you want to."

"I got him on a claim and, sooner or later, I'm going to lose him that way." I shrugged. "It might as well be today. Let's hope he wins."

"That's how I feel about it, as well," replied Robert. "There are lots of other similar horses out there. Let's hope for a win. I don't understand this thing about claiming horses. Could you go over it once more for me?"

"I'd be happy to," I said. "It's the way the track officials set up the races so that they get as many horses of the same quality in each race. There are different kinds of races. In claiming races, you are chancing that someone will 'claim' your horse away from you for the price set in the race, for instance five thousand dollars. That means anyone who has raced or trained a horse that has run on this track can buy the horse from you, and you have no recourse except to scratch him or take him out of the race before the race starts.

"Then there are conditioned races. That means your horse has to meet the conditions of the race or he can't be entered to run. The conditions might be for non-winners of two races this year. If your horse hasn't won this year, he can be entered. If he has won once this year that's okay, as well. The track officials know what horses are being kept here and others around that could be entered. That's how they try to make it possible for several horses to win."

The fifth race was called shortly, so we went out to watch my old boy, to see if he could get around in all the mud.

Will tried to get him out front from the five hole, but he was getting old and couldn't manage it. He had to settle for second at the rail. On the back stretch, Will urged him to try for the lead as the lead horse seemed to be taking a breather. They got in just in time for the clubhouse turn—the other four horses were having a hard time of it and Kingston Kenny stayed in front to the end. I had a winner, our second of the day.

This time we had no time for another coffee as the sixth race was announced, so we went back out to watch Sam's Friend do his best. There were only four horses in this race, as the others who were originally supposed to run had been scratched because of the mud.

Will, again, went the front. At least that way our horse wasn't continually getting mud and water kicked in his face. Horses loved to run and be the leader of the pack, but after a mile of mud some got discouraged.

The strategy worked and we had our third winner of the day but lost all our horses to claims. That's life; we could get some cheap claimers or maybe some untried young horses at the sales at a later date. For now, we would just pack our bags and see what my old friend in Smith's Falls had on his mind.

Sunday, Morag, my housekeeper, made roast beef for lunch. As usual, there was way too much food—in the way of vegetables and desserts, in particular. George and Robert came over as always. They lived alone, as did I, and this was our favourite day to just relax together. It was a bit early in the season to go fishing yet. I guess we could have tried for catfish; they, at least, were in season, but we had decided not to bother.

After lunch, Robert went off to fly his beloved Spitfire. He did a lot of airshows with it. I called both of my sons on the phone to check that they were still on for our semiannual get-together. We always enjoyed these visits. Their families got along well together.

We had been stuck in the house most of the winter. We planned to get to Toronto soon to see how Bert Mason, our trainer there, was doing with our horses. Nor had we been able to get to Chapleau to visit our friend Marie and her family. Her sister Betty, and Betty's husband, Dan, lived with her, and they had become a close group. We would have to fit in some visits soon. But first it was off to see my old roommate.

Monday, we went to the airport, got the plane ready and flew to Smith's Falls.

CHAPTER 2

My friend Bruce had told me his phone number, but there had been no answer when I called from the airport, so we sat down to have a light meal in town.

"He has an old farm east of town," I told my companions. "I don't know whether he wants us to stay at his place or in town here. When I get him on the phone, I'll ask him what his plans are."

There was a pay phone on the wall of the restaurant, so as our food was being prepared, I tried dialing him again.

"No, I want you and your friends to stay here," said Bruce. "I have room for you. I've added some cottages to the property over the past four or five years. I'll send my assistant to pick you up after lunch, say about 1:00 p.m. Her name is Sue McGregor. She's a good-looking blonde, so leave her alone," said Bruce. "See you soon."

Sue picked us up as promised. Like Bruce said, she was a nice-looking girl. Within fifteen minutes we arrived at his place. It was previously a small dairy farm. Now the property boasted several buildings—more than the original farmer had owned—including a main barn that was bigger than any barn I'd ever seen, and several small, cottage-type structures.

Sue drove up to a large cabin and there was my friend Bruce Monfils to welcome us. I jumped out of the car and grabbed Bruce's hand, shaking it vigorously. We hadn't seen each other is several years.

"What have you got here?" I exclaimed. "It's like a small village!"

"I guess it is, in a way," said Bruce, laughing. "It started off as a small farm, but things kind of got out of hand, especially recently. There are quite a few people who spend a lot of time here. This cabin over here has three bedrooms—if you have no objections, I was thinking the three of you could stay here."

"That sounds fine to me," I said. "Let me introduce my friends. This big fellow here is my friend George Kingman, and the other good-looking guy is Robert Mackie."

"Well, I'm very pleased to make your acquaintance," said Bruce. "Now put your baggage in here and we'll go over to the house, and I'll explain what's going on."

When we were all settled with a coffee and a couple of biscuits each at Bruce's kitchen table, Bruce took a deep sigh and began his tale.

"I hope you fellows are prepared for a long story," said Bruce. "By the way, how long can you stay?"

"We came prepared to stay awhile," I said. "You sounded like you needed us to help you with something. We have nothing to keep us busy, so we're here for however long it takes."

"That's good, but, most important, I have to ask you to keep mum about what I'm about to share with you."

Robert, George, and I looked at each other and shrugged. "Sure. Go on and tell us," I said.

"It all started about fifteen years ago," began Bruce. "I was at the University of Toronto and sort of looking into waves in space and other things. I discovered something that, to me, just didn't add up right. I was reviewing a paper on the Higgs boson, an atomic particle.

It didn't look like anything significant. At first, I just thought I made a mistake in my math somewhere. But when I started looking at dark matter, which makes up most of our universe, then things just started falling into place. Whatever that means . . .

"Anyway, the more I thought about it, the more peculiar it struck me as. Then the war came along and many of us were recruited to research anything that might help the war effort. This project didn't look too promising in that way, but since the government was paying, we just kept at it. The war ended without us getting very far, but we had learned to control things a little. It was very intriguing, so I left my university job and decided to devote myself to this discovery full time. That's when I bought the farm.

"You may recall my family was quite well off. I have since inherited everything and have put it all into this project. It's now starting to pay dividends, but not financially, so I need some volunteer labour. That's where you come in.

"This energy I've discovered—or whatever you want to call it—appears to let us open what you might call a 'door' or 'gate' to another world or dimension, or something."

"I don't believe it," said George. "How could that be?"

"You'll just have to be patient," said Bruce. "I hope to be able to explain it to you a little more before I show you what I'm talking about. You can then decide for yourself. I just ask that you don't mention this to anyone else for now. I've tried several times to talk to academia since going on my own but got laughed out of the room, so until we have more proof, I'd like to keep it under wraps. What I need you guys to do is some of the grunt work in setting up different kinds of experiments for me."

"I meant to ask you how you found me after all these years," I said. "We had lost touch before the war."

"My neighbour," Bruce replied. "He has some horses he races, and he sometimes uses them as an excuse for a holiday from the farm. Last fall he raced one in Peterborough and beat a horse owned by you. He was quite proud of the fact. After the race he was talking to you and your friends here, and you invited him and his wife to your cottage to go fishing."

"You must be talking about Albert and Bonnie Black!" I said. "Very nice folks. You say they're your neighbours?"

"They own the farm to the west of us."

I turned to Robert and George and said, "We'll have to go visit them while we're here."

"They help us here, now and then, and we've bought some experimental animals from them. A couple of cows and pigs, and a half dozen chickens," said Bruce.

"You've certainly piqued my curiosity," said Robert.

"The Blacks told us about your lifestyle and what you do," said Bruce, "and then I followed up because of the name and discovered that it really was you. I have need of what you might call 'adventurers' or 'explorers' to help me with my work here. You fit the mould beautifully and I know you well and feel I can trust you, even though we haven't seen each other in a while.

"You'll have to take what I say at face value for a while. Like I said, this . . . force, or whatever you might call it, opens a door to another dimension, we think. It's very much like our planet here, but very different as well. Let's go out to the barn and I'll show you what I mean."

As we walked out to the barn, Bruce pointed out Albert and Bonnie's farm. "I told them you would be coming," said Bruce. "They're anxious to say hello."

We walked into the building, which Bruce explained was just a big barn with some machines at one end. It was very quiet inside.

"Why such a big building if you only need that space at the back?" asked Robert.

"Good question," said Bruce. "At first we thought our experiment might result in some explosions or something like that, so I built it solid and big enough to contain anything. Nothing like that has ever happened, but this place is certainly solid. The main structure is reinforced concrete, even the roof. Then we worried it might have to hold other things. That was after we happened upon the gateway. We've found, though, that this world we got through to is very empty. It is very similar to Earth but doesn't have any life that we've found yet and we are now into our fifth year of exploration.

"By the way, I say 'exploring' but we haven't ventured far from base. If you agree, I'd love for you to expand our horizons." Bruce had been fiddling with some switches and controls on the wall while he talked.

A low hum started up and suddenly the back wall disappeared, and a wild-looking landscape appeared where the back wall had been. "As near as we can figure, we are now connected to a different world. The composition of the elements in the air are almost identical, and the water is the same, as well, but does have some things in it that are not found in water on our planet."

A horn had gone off and a three-foot-high barrier had come up all around the door. Two guys with high powered rifles had appeared from a small room and taken up position on either side. "That barrier and the guards are just in case this world is not as empty as it seems. None of us has ever seen or heard anything from inside, but no one knows for certain. We have a couple of cows in an enclosure and a couple of pigs, as well as a little flock of chickens living in there.

They all seem to like it and nothing has disturbed them as far as we can tell.

"I remembered you were a pilot in the war, which is another reason I got in touch. We have a plane to help us explore in more depth."

"All three of us are pilots," I said.

"All the better," replied Bruce. "We have a Cessna 180 that's been modified in several ways. It has been stripped and extra fuel has been added, and it's also been converted to burn ethanol. Over the years we've tried growing several crops in the new environment, and corn is one of them. They grow quite well. We've also tried fish in the lake, and they do well, too. The place seems to be devoid of predators."

We walked out into the field. "That's a pine and an oak," exclaimed George. "And it looks like a couple of maples over there. They're not very big yet but for only five years I'd say they've grown nicely."

"They are what you think they are. The first year we did some planting and as you can see, the trees have done well. Now we need to expand our boundaries—that's where you three can help us."

"Is this the plane?" asked Robert, patting the Cessna we were standing beside.

"Yes, we had a pilot to fly it, but he was in a car accident last year and was killed. The plane has just been sitting here since. We do have an aircraft mechanic who performs regular safety checks."

"Do you mind if I look it over?" said Robert. "I'd love to take it up, if that's all right."

"That's the idea," said Bruce. "That's what it's here for. There are no flying rules here, so it's ready when you are."

"Robert is the best pilot of the three of us," I explained to Bruce. "I'll let him take the lead. How about fuel, ethanol? It's not that easy to come by."

"We have plenty for now," Bruce explained. "We got a large distillery to see if we could make our own fuel. It's stored in that big plastic tank over there. I picked up a couple of surplus army jeeps and we converted one of them. Stripped of all the armor, it can go quite a long way on a tank of ethanol"

Some fellow called to Bruce that he was needed for some sort of crisis, so he hurried off, leaving us to our own devices.

"We might as well check out this plane while we're here," said Robert. "Why don't we all give it a thorough walk-around preflight, then start it up to see what we have?"

"Good idea," agreed George, "walk-around first, then while you run it up, Ron and I will see if we can set up some kind of runway." The walk-around looked good; the mechanic must have been thorough. Robert got in and looked things over. "Good set of instruments," he said. "Stand back, I'm going to see if she'll start." It started with a roar and settled down nicely to a steady hum. The plane ran well.

George and I started off in different directions to see if we could map out a bit of a runway. The land looked nice and level in most directions: to the east was a rocky, mountainous area, which stretched north and south quite extensively. A watercourse could be seen west of the rocky area. George and I both walked several hundred yards in the directions we had chosen. George had gone south, and I west. Both directions were fine for a runway. We went back to the plane and talked to Robert.

"The plane is a beauty," said Robert. "What did you find by way of a runway?"

"Both directions appear to be great, no problems, not even big stones," I reported.

"Hardly any stones, big or small," added George. "The terrain is almost like a grassy lawn."

Let's go back to the house and talk about strategy," said Robert. "I'd say everything is a go for early tomorrow, but we should clear it with Bruce."

As we walked back to the barn, George said, "This is all a dream, a fairy tale. I can see why the academic community laughed at your friend. Who in their right mind could imagine such a thing? Yet, here we are, accepting all this as normal."

"It truly is unbelievable," I said. "But here we are living it. I think we need to just accept things as we see them."

Bruce was standing by the main farmhouse talking to some people. "These people here are a couple of our 'big brains,'" he said to us. "Mary is our resident expert on the universe and Peter is a leading plant specialist. These are my old friends, Ron, George, and Robert—they will be piloting our plane and exploring our new environment by air. We're going to have supper in a few minutes; I'm glad you returned just now. Bonnie and Albert are coming over from their farm to eat with us. Bonnie has promised us some of her world-famous apple pie for dessert."

We asked Bruce what he would like us to do tomorrow.

"You're in charge," he said, "just go ahead and explore at your pace, but keep us in the loop. Map things out if you can, that's what we need most right now."

Albert and Bonnie's pickup came rattling up the driveway and when they hopped out of the truck, there was a good-old reunion. Bonnie had brought a couple of her apple pies. Mary and Peter showed their appreciation by praising the pies. We all headed inside.

"You haven't met half the people who live here yet," said Bruce. "I'm afraid I went a bit overboard in a lot of ways. I just want to prove to all the doubting Thomases who laughed at me what an incredible discovery we've made here. The main trouble is we're starting to overflow in several ways. I'll tell you about it over dinner."

Bruce led us to a large dining room that would seat about twenty people. The food was laid out like a buffet. All the dishes were set out on a long side table and we were told to help ourselves to whatever we wanted. Large quantities of many different types of meats and vegetables were there for our consumption.

"How can you afford all this?" I exclaimed. "I knew you were rich, but this is preposterous."

"Believe it or not, this costs me next to nothing," said Bruce. "It's all compliments of how we are set up, and it's part of the problem."

"How could this be a problem?" I asked. "These vegetables look fresh and delicious."

"When we started, we set up a couple of small farms, I guess you'd call them, on the new planet. We put three cattle, all dairy, in one area, with some pigs and chickens nearby. Then we set up a sort of market garden, with ordinary vegetables, just to see how they would do. Two couples of Albert's acquaintance had recently lost their farms, due to the Depression and war. They had no jobs and nowhere to go, so we built a couple of small houses near the enclosures, and they do all the farming.

"The experiment has been almost too successful. You can see the proof right here at the table. You might say that the land is too pure, everything grows and reproduces in rapid, enormous quantities. We give away as much as we can and we eat well and we still have too much. And the taste is better—you might say, out of this world! People are starting to get suspicious!

"I've had to hire extra bodies for help with planting, harvesting and building the structures. That's been no problem—we rescued a couple of vets from the street who were suffering from shell shock. They've taken to their new life well; they like the quiet peacefulness. They're super handymen—one guy knows electronics and the other is a jack-leg plumber.

"They live on-site on the other planet. Very soon, I'll need to hire a couple more workers. Basically, they need to be willing to work for room and board, which, as I say, is nothing. One of the couples who run the main farm has recently gotten into beekeeping, it's going well. Lots of honey. The flowers and apple trees need pollination."

"You've certainly got a tiger by the tail," I said. "What are you going to do about it?"

"What I've decided is to release all our findings come fall and see where the chips fall."

Albert came over to say that he had a horse running in Ottawa on Friday night and invited us to come watch him run.

"Sounds like a great idea," I said. "I think there are two tracks in Ottawa, are there not?"

"No, just one, but there is another across the river in Gatineau, Quebec," said Albert.

"Count us in for sure," I answered.

CHAPTER 3

Bonnie drove us to the track on Friday, while Albert drove the horse transport, carrying two horses.

"The drivers at both Ottawa and Gatineau don't like outsiders racing on their track," said Bonnie. "We're not considered 'one of them.' But they don't dare try anything with Albert around—he's a pretty big fellow for them to take on. We usually get a fair reception, maybe because we don't pose too much of a threat to their winning."

"I saw Albert load two horses," said George. "What are their names, so we can cheer for them?"

"The young filly is Sunshine Sally; she's new to racing, this will be her first race. The ninth is a race for maidens, so we got her in to see what she can do. She's been training well. The gelding is eight years old and has been around for a while; his name is Broadway Jack. He's in a claimer, but he's only middle of the pack in ability. He just likes to run."

We got a small tour of the clubhouse; it was a nice facility. Albert came over from the barns after he had unloaded. He was very agitated.

"They started in on me as soon as I arrived!" he exclaimed loudly. "Three of them surrounded me and started asking me questions about Sunshine Sally. Then they told me, in no uncertain terms, that she would not win her race. I told them that she had a chance like all the others, then they got very threatening. They didn't do anything, but it got kind of intense for a few minutes."

"Is there anything we can do to help?" I asked.

"No, I don't think so," said Albert. "I expect it's all just a big noise over nothing, but it's upsetting. I have to get back over there—I had to get away to blow off a little steam. See you later."

Broadway Jack started slow and didn't improve much as the race went on. Sunshine Sally was in the last race. She started off a bit slow and was boxed in most of the way, but she got out late and looked like she was going to make a nice run at the leader then slowed up suddenly and broke stride to finish second last. We waited in the parking lot for Albert and the horses. He was raging when he joined us.

"Can you wait a while?" he asked. "I need to have a word with the officials. Those drivers over there nobbled both horses. I've got a witness. A fellow came to me when I got back from talking to you before the races. He said he saw a couple of guys with a twitch feed something to Broadway Jack—he thinks they had a couple of shakers of salt. Then they gave him a couple of buckets of water to drink. No wonder he couldn't get going."

"He wouldn't be able to do his best with all that water sloshing around inside him," I said. "We'll wait. Do you want one of us to come with you?"

"No, I'll be all right. You can go on back to the farm. I'll catch up with your there." With that, he strode across to the main office.

When Albert got back, we sat down to a cup of coffee to listen to the sorry tale of the night's racing.

"I sort of expected something like this might happen," said Albert. "They've hinted at it before; they must be getting desperate. The officials said they saw nothing odd in the last race. Poor old Sally . . . when she started her run, she was doing well for a few strides and gaining speed. We had a horse on each side of us and when we went to pass, they used their whips on her, she got frightened and broke stride. What a way to start her career, poor little lady."

"I didn't see what they did to her," I said, "just noticed her break stride."

"What they did to Jack was pure stupidity; they were seen. The officials said they would look into it, so I guess we'll just have to wait."

"All we can do now is forget about it," said Bonnie. "There's a good movie on in town tomorrow. Why don't we all go see that?"

"What movie is it?" George asked.

"It's science fiction—kind of appropriate I think—and a bit scary," said Bonnie. "It's called *The Time Machine.* It's about a guy who invents a time machine and goes way ahead in time."

"Sounds a bit like our situation," said Robert. "Let's do it."

Saturday's breakfast consisted of bacon, eggs, toast, home fries, coffee—and lots of all of it.

"All this comes from our farm—the out-planet farm, that is," said Bruce.

"What do you do with all the excess?" I asked.

"Much of it gets fed to the pigs on the farms—they love it and grow fat quickly. Most of the rest is composted. The problem is the pigs breed quickly and that leaves us with even more bacon and pork. We've been selling it off quietly to several places, which gives us a nice profit, but it's a lot of extra work we don't need.

"Another thing you'll notice is the jam you see here. One of the ladies at the farm is a dab hand at making it. We sell the jam and a lot of fruit and vegetables at a stand out on the highway. The farm people handle that, but we must be careful that we sell only in-season stuff. Since we produce all year round, that's another problem. We can't go on this way much longer, but we'll keep going while we can."

"The taste is different as well," I said. "Better taste all around, in my opinion, but certainly different."

"Different soil chemistry I expect," said Bruce. "I agree with you, though; I like the taste better. I probably eat too much as a result. I've hired another veteran to market those things, as well as our milk. We've accumulated a rather large herd since we put the first cattle there five years ago. We've since added a small beef herd. We bring the milk through every day and a truck picks it up here."

Lunch and dinner were both blessed with more food than we needed with leftover pie from last night for dessert. Bonnie and Albert picked us up early and we went to the theatre in town to watch *The Time Machine.*

"Our situation is different," said Bonnie, on the way home. "I liked the little group of non-offensive people called the Eloi. Such a horrible fate being killed and eaten by the Morlocks."

Robert, George and I went to church Sunday at the First Baptist church in Smith's Falls. It was situated on the main street, with three or four other churches of different denominations clustered close around. After the opening prayer, the pastor immediately asked for volunteers to search the town for a missing teenage girl. She hadn't come home Saturday night and the parents were very worried.

Pastor Stead's sermon was called "Discipleship: Like Jesus," the main theme being that every problem has a purpose.

After the service, the three of us went to the town hall and were given a part of town to search. We were told to particularly check backyards and alleys. We searched the area we were assigned and went back to the control centre, only to find the girl had been found raped and strangled. She appeared to have been dragged down the railroad tracks to an area near the old detached lock and the cantilever railroad bridge.

We were reassigned an area near the bridge to go over very carefully to see if we could find anything that might be tied to the crime. The police were overworked and had no clues at all. When we had scoured our small section three times, we went back to the officer in charge. Robert and I had found nothing. George had found a paper matchbook with all the matches gone.

"It's not much of a clue, I guess," said George, "but it looks new. It's not weathered, and it's from the Russell Hotel in town."

"Anything helps," said the constable. "Quite often it's the little things. We don't get these kinds of happenings around here very often. It's a nice, quiet place to live."

We walked dejectedly back to the car that Bruce had lent us and drove back to the farm to tell the people.

Monday, we started to work in earnest. Robert did the preflight test while George and I checked out the radios. The radio was radically different than what we were used to. Bruce had bought four of a new kind. They were called single sideband—a new concept, recently developed to reach farther with less power.

I was to look after the base while George went with Robert. They were going to try their hand at mapping, timing their flight with direction and airspeed noted. I was to keep in constant touch and serve as a direction indicator if they needed it to get home. They went about an hour, what they thought was 200 nautical miles, then turned east, flew half an hour, and used my base radio as a direction beacon to turn for home.

After the flight we put our heads together to map out what we had. George had made sketches at various spots and he and Robert roughed in the surrounding area as best they could. This was our first try so there were lots of gaps. We broke for lunch and went back to the farm.

"That wasn't a lot of work," said Robert, "but if we can do a twenty-five-degree sector of sorts, by flying 200 nautical miles every morning and afternoon, we can complete a 400 nautical mile circle in less than a week."

"I heard that," said Bruce, joining us at the table for lunch. "That's a huge advance on what we know"

"What's the main objective here?" I asked.

"We want to know a lot more about this place is all at the moment," said Bruce. "We don't have any concrete plans—we just keep expanding. We can't expand too much more though; I'm starting to run out of funds. Selling off the excess farm products helps a little. Our stargazers managed to buy a complete stellar observatory, a small one that was being torn down at a university out west. It'll be shipped here by tomorrow. Then we have to figure out where and how we set it up. Your map will help with that.

"Also, one of our people heard about a metal fencing company going out of business and we acquired a huge amount of excess fencing stock, enough for years. I guess it's about time that we made the world believe. The politicians will probably take over and do what they want. We'll lose everything, but maybe we can keep a small part to ourselves. For now, just keep plugging away at what you're doing until we lose hold of everything."

"I personally need to take next week off for my annual family reunion, but I'll be back with bells on immediately afterward," I said. "I have two boys who are grown with families, and we do this every year."

"That's no problem," said Bruce, "we're not in any rush. Take whatever time off you need."

"I've got a fortune myself, so if you need money for anything, just ask."

"That's very generous," said Bruce.

"Off the topic," said Robert, "these vegetables are the best I've ever eaten. The potatoes taste like those new potatoes you can get in early spring, they're fabulous."

"Like I said before," replied Bruce, "I think it's due to the different soil chemistry. Maybe one of the big brains we have hanging around here could give you a better answer, but that's mine."

We went back to mapping for the afternoon with the same manpower alignment. To pass the time and as a check, I made notes of the observations that George radioed back. At times they would come upon a distinctive land feature. They came across a very big river mid-afternoon. Going by how long it took them to fly across, it must have been close to six miles wide. Making note of these discoveries took up the time and helped with the boredom of just sitting there.

Conversation at Monday's supper mostly focused on the young girl's murder. Police had gotten nowhere with their investigation. We sat down to a giant roast of beef, enough to feed everyone present. It was seasoned just right for my taste and very tender, well marbled. The vegetables were many and varied, tasting delicious as usual.

The rest of the week we continued our mapping efforts. By the end of the week we had a rough map. Good for about 200 nautical miles in all directions, showing the main rivers, lakes, hills and valleys.

Wednesday, we went to Albert and Bonnie's for supper. The meal was excellent, capped off with lemon pie, my favourite.

During dinner, Albert said, "That murder has really shaken up the town; we know the family, they're very stressed. She was a good girl, they had never had any problems with her. She was not the best scholar, but very sweet."

"Knowing the person involved just adds to the tragedy," I said. "It makes my blood boil when I hear about something like that happening. To be that close by hits you hard."

When we arrived at the plane for our Thursday morning flight, the mechanic was waiting for us.

"I don't think we were introduced," he said, "my name is Frank Howard. I'd like to join you here for the job you're doing. I don't have an official pilot's license, but I can fly. What I can contribute is an artistic hand for the maps you're making."

"Pleased to meet you, Frank. My name is Ron. I guess we could use you," I said. "We'll take you up this morning on our first flight, then we can talk about it over lunch"

"My name is George," said George. "I'm flying co-pilot and timing things. This here's Robert. He's our best pilot, so he'll do the actual flying."

"Nice to meet you, Frank," said Robert.

"Thank you for the opportunity," said Frank. "I need to get away. My first cousin was raped and killed last week, and it's been bothering me a lot."

"My condolences," I said. "I didn't know you were related."

"We weren't very close, but it's been all I can think about," he said.

"I can only imagine," I said. "I'm sure it would disturb me a great deal."

Robert and George both did the preflight checks with Frank trailing along. They then took off on their pre-decided route for today's flight. I was manning the radio again; George promised that next week, he would spell me in that boring occupation, while I joined the flight crew to do the timing and mapping.

The morning was at least punctuated by the arrival of a large transport truck loaded with rolled-up fencing. The driver took the rig over to the small mountains to the west. They were about a mile and a half away, but not very high; they rose perhaps a thousand feet, consisting of very rough-looking rock. The local geography was quite flat, but it rose to the north to a plateau of a good size. A large lake stretched out to the west of that. Near the lake the land rose rapidly to this plateau, about twenty-five feet higher than the lake. At this south end of the lake was a waterfall about a total of thirty feet high. The falls dropped into a river heading south. We had been using the near bank as our landing field. The river was about half a mile wide, and slow-flowing.

It took the driver all morning to unload, but he came back near lunchtime with an empty truck. He had been too far away from me for me to see what he was unloading.

Lunch was more like dinner in terms of the amount of food that was on hand. I was sitting with Bruce again, so I said, "There was a truck that came into the new world this morning loaded with wire. Are you expanding that much more?"

"I made a bit of a mistake," said Bruce. "I bought what I thought were the assets of a small fencing company which was going bankrupt.

It turns out they weren't that small. We did need a little more wire, but this is more than we can use. You'll see several other trucks over the next few days. I think I mentioned that Mary managed to get hold of an old observatory telescope that was being replaced at a university out west. It's being shipped here.

"We'd like to get as much info on this planet as we can. As you probably noticed it has two moons, so we were actually thinking of calling it 'Two Moons,' since we don't have a name for it yet. It is very similar to Earth—that's the kind of planet this gadget of mine seems to pick up. Similar in air, water and soil composition, as well as axial tilt. The climate seems temperate—no snow or cold temperatures, but we do get some rain. There was, at one time, a volcano just over in those rocky hills to the east, but we haven't had time to explore very much. That's why we need you and your friends."

"When you say that's the kind of planet your gadget picks up, do you mean there are others?"

"Oh, yes, at least four or five, but they're not quite as Earth-like. The differences are not substantial, but this is the best one for farming—that's why we chose to develop it first. I hope to have it as developed as possible in a couple of months so that I can show and convince academia of what we have here. A gateway to the stars."

"Well, we'll be back as soon as we can. Is it okay if I bring my boat back with me so I can look at the other side of the river?"

"Sure, bring anything that you think will help."

We hopped in the old jeep and drove back to the plane. George, Robert and Frank headed out for another sector sweep. I stayed in the jeep and drove toward the rocky hills. I was surprised at their extent; they were a lot bigger and more imposing up close. There were several large caves along the base. The driver of the big truck returned with another load of fencing.

"How much fencing have you got?" I asked

"Another couple of loads should do it," he replied. "A lot more than we thought."

"Were you the fellow here this morning?"

"Yes, I'm the only one allowed to bring stuff in. Other drivers bring the goods to the farm, and I bring it the rest of the way—that way rumours don't get started."

Friday afternoon the three of us flew back to Peterborough.

CHAPTER 4

Malcolm, my youngest son, Sandra, his wife, and their two children, twelve-year-old Barry and nine-year-old Denise, arrived shortly after we got back to Peterborough on Friday night. Morag had their rooms ready and dinner on the table. All we had to do was sit down and eat. After dinner, we had a rousing game of Monopoly, which Malcolm won. He was an accountant, so it only made sense that he was good at that sort of game. Barry and Denise were chips off the old block. Like their dad, they did very well. I, on the other hand, finished the game bankrupt.

Morag always made a hearty breakfast on Saturday and Sunday. Today was no exception. We had been finished for about an hour when my other son, James, arrived with June and their two girls, Sandra, age ten, and Sharon, eight. All four of my grandchildren were at that age that they loved to play board games, so another game of Monopoly was started almost immediately. We put a time limit of two hours on the game so we could get outside. We wanted to visit the zoo. All the children were eager to see the new additions.

A barbeque was planned as the main part of the party, later in the day. Morag was preparing the food, along with a cake for dessert.

We did this as a family at least once a year and even though we got together individually more often than that, this was an annual event we all looked forward to. On Sunday, the whole family went to church and for a nice long walk after. In the afternoon, we went to John's farm to see the horses. Will and Max got the children on the sulky to take them for rides around the track.

John was enthusiastic about buying new horses for the new year. "You'll have to get at least a new horse each," said John. "The ones you have now are getting old—another year and they'll have to stop because of their age. I'll look for some replacements for you. The best thing would be for you to go to the spring sales in Toronto while you're there. They have lots of horses—some that have raced previously and some yearlings."

"Thanks," I said, "we had already decided to do just that. Dave, my assistant trainer has been looking over what is available. That's the first thing we intend to do."

It was time for everyone to head home after the visit to the farm. The kids, in particular, had enjoyed themselves—the drives around the track in the sulky being their favourite part of the trip.

George and Robert had flown to the cottage. George was going to bring the boat back to take to Smith's Falls. Sunday night rolled around and we all thought the weekend had flown by far too quickly.

Monday, George and Robert were back in Peterborough. We had previously planned to go see our friends in both Toronto and Chapleau. George had brought the boat with one of the canoes on top. We parked that in my driveway and hopped in the plane to fly to Chapleau. We hadn't seen our friends there all winter and we wanted to get in some fishing, as well.

Dan, our friend Marie's brother-in-law, met us at the airport and drove us all out to Marie's place.

Even the dogs were glad to see us. Irish wolfhounds are big dogs; it's a good thing if they like you. Currently Marie owned five of the wolfhounds. Too many mouths to feed, in my opinion, but it seemed like everything was well in their world. We had a good visit, then George and Robert went fishing with Marie's son, Jimmy, while I went out in another boat with Dan.

"How are things in general?" I asked Dan.

"Marie is coping better now without Serge. As you know, she had a hard time of it mentally after he was killed. Jimmy is growing fast, as you can see. He's a good help for her. Betty and I have settled in nicely. We're expecting again. We have a good life here."

Dan and I each caught a nice pickerel while, as usual, Jimmy led Robert and George to the big ones. They had each managed to land a large muskie. We had a nice fish fry for supper.

"Will you three help us with a deer hunt tomorrow?" said Dan. "I know it's out of season so you can't help with the shooting, but you could take the dogs and circle to drive the deer to us. That would help a lot. We really need dog food."

"We can do that all right but who will be doing the shooting?" I replied.

"Just me and Jimmy," said Dan

"Well, I guess Jimmy is in his teens now," I said

"He's a crack shot," said Dan. "He never misses."

Next morning, we hopped into the boat and went over to the far side of the lake where they always hunted. Jimmy and Dan set up in their spots to wait; George took one dog and headed out in one direction, Robert took another dog in a second direction, and I headed out with a third dog. When we were about a mile out, we started to circle, making some noise and closing in toward our shooters. About twenty minutes later we heard first one gunshot go off, then another shot being fired. I headed toward where I thought Jimmy was. Altogether, there were three shots in rapid succession: the signal that someone was in trouble. The shots came from Jimmy's direction. I broke into a rough jog, the best I could manage though the heavy brush. Jimmy was standing in the clearing. He didn't seem upset; he just pointed off to the side. There was a dead scruffy-looking old bear on the ground not far from him.

"He came out of nowhere," said Jimmy. "He was after my deer then he charged me. I would never have been able to outrun him; all I could do was shoot him."

Dan had arrived in time to hear the conversation.

"You did right," said Dan. "Did it take three shots to down him?"

"I hit him all three times," said Jimmy. "He just kept coming. Last time he stood up to come at me and I got him really good."

"That was very brave to stand your ground like that," I said. "Many people would have panicked."

"He must have been quite strong," said Jimmy. "I know I hit him all three times. I guess he was hungry and desperate for the deer."

"He's an old fellow," said Dan, "and look at that forefoot. He must have caught it in a trap. He was crippled; no wonder he wanted your deer. The dogs like bear meat so we have a good harvest to take home. Our dogs are big enough to carry most of it back to the boats."

Robert and George had come into the clearing while we were talking. "I'll start working on cleaning out the bear," said George.

"I'll help," said Robert.

"I think I'll go back to my deer before we get any more unwanted surprises," said Dan. "I'll bring it over here when I'm finished."

"Well, I can either help Jimmy or I can help with the bear," I said.

"I'm okay with the deer," said Jimmy. "Help with the bear—that's a big job."

"Bear it is," I said. "I'll start skinning it."

Altogether, we had a large amount of meat, plenty enough for a month or two. We loaded the dogs and shouldered some ourselves for the trek back to the lake. It was a stretch, everyone carrying all they could. The boat was fully loaded for the trip home across the lake.

We were pretty grungy after dressing the deer and bear so we opted to fly back to Peterborough. A luxurious shower and clean-up helped with my disposition at least. No doubt Robert and George felt the same. After spending the night at home, we flew to Toronto to see our friends the Gransdens and check out the horses. Both Dave and Leslie were at home having a coffee on the porch when we arrived on their doorstep.

"Good to see you!" said Dave. "We've mapped out several horses you may be interested in. John phoned last week to tell us you lost all three of your horses to claims, so I started to look for replacements for you."

"Sounds good," I said. "How is the veterinarian course coming, Leslie?"

"I'm finally done," she replied. "I get my diploma in large animals next month. I originally thought that I wanted to open a practice in Bobcaygeon, but my parents tell me two others have opened up there this year, so I'm not sure what I'll do now."

"I won't be able to look after your horses if we move," added Dave. "And Toronto is no place for a large animal vet. I'd like our kids to grow up someplace other than a big city."

"You're quite right; you need to be living in a small town or the country now that you have the two little ones. We'll work something out. We're visiting a friend near Smith's Falls just now—maybe there's a need for a vet there. We'll check next week, and I'll let you know. Let's go look at some of these horses that you mentioned."

The horse auction and sale were scheduled for the evening, so we had an early supper at their favourite restaurant, a buffet in the east end.

Our Toronto trainer, Bert Mason, was there to help. "There's a really fine colt that I'd like to buy, but I can't afford him," he said. "I was wondering if you could buy him for me to train."

"I'd be willing to look at him and if he's as good as you say then I'd love to have him, and you can give it your best shot. I presume he would be in the classic stakes category."

"Oh, yes," he said. "He comes from one of the best breeders."

We bought four horses in the end, plus the colt that our trainer liked. More than we planned, but they were a good price. There were lots of others there, but the prices were out of our league.

Robert liked a young gelding that he felt was within his budget, so he bid on it and got it. He was back in racing, having only ever had the horse he lost in the claiming race. He'd made the decision to buy the horse all by himself. He liked to be independent.

We got two young fillies with what seemed to be good upside from where they were competing currently, an older gelding who was a consistent runner, and a young colt that the breeder had given up on for some reason. He looked quite sound even though the breeder was no longer interested.

I called John, my trainer in Peterborough, and arranged for Will to pick up our new horses.

We stayed overnight and flew back to Peterborough next morning. George and Robert flew on to Smith's Falls while I stayed overnight and then took the boats and trailer next morning and drove them to the farm in Smith's Falls and through to Two Moons.

On arrival at Two Moons, George and Robert came over to say hello.

"Hi," I said. "How come you're here to greet me? Don't you trust me to get here on my own?"

"Well, it's like this," said George. "What if you had broken down? We would then have had to go rescue you. Didn't you ever hear of the older man who was driving along in his beat-up old Dodge, when suddenly it broke down? He was parked on the side of the road trying to fix it, when a Jaguar pulled up in front of him and offered to help. After a few minutes of trying, the two men were obviously not going to get the old Dodge going again, so the Jaguar driver offered to tow the Dodge to the nearest garage. A few minutes later, the two had hitched up the old Dodge to the Jaguar. They agreed that if the Jaguar driver was going too fast, the man should blow his horn and flash his lights to get him to slow down. With that, the two men got in their cars and the Jaguar driver started to pull away with the Dodge behind it.

"At the first traffic light, a Ferrari pulled up beside the Jaguar. The Ferrari started revving his engine provocatively. As soon as the light turned green, the Ferrari and the Jaguar hit their accelerators and took off. Before long, the cars were racing along at over 120 miles per hour. As the cars sped along, they passed through a police speed trap. The officer couldn't believe his eyes when he saw the three cars go by. He decided he couldn't catch them all by himself, so he decided to radio for help. 'You won't believe what I saw! I saw a Jaguar and a Ferrari doing 120 miles per hour side by side, and a beat-up old Dodge behind them flashing his lights and blowing his horn trying to get by!"

We laughed. "That's good, George," I said. "I do get myself into some predicaments at times."

We took the boat to the water and anchored it to a rock on the shore. We put the canoe alongside. “Now we can try out the fishing,” I said. “I’ve been dying to give it a try. It’s been over five years since Bruce stocked this area with fish. They should be a good size.”

“Good idea,” said Robert. “We haven’t had much time to relax here yet. First break we get I’m all for some fishing action.”

The drive had taken me all day. Supper was ready and I was famished.

CHAPTER 5

While we were away for the week, another young teenage girl had been attacked in Smith's Falls. Peter, the plant specialist, came over during dinner.

"I thought I saw you bring in a boat today," he said. "Is there any possibility of me borrowing it to get to the other side of the river?"

"Yes, of course," I said. "I brought a canoe and a fishing boat with a ten-horsepower motor. The motor hasn't been converted to ethanol yet; you have to use a gas/oil mixture. If you're unsure how to do it, just ask. You can borrow either."

"Thank you," he said. "I'd like to see how some plants take to the other side."

"Let's take a walk around town," I said to Robert and George after dinner. "We can see if there is anything suspicious looking, and it's a nice night for a walk. We should be doing this every night since we seem to have a serial rapist on the loose."

We drove to town and parked by the small café on Main Street. We each set out in a different direction, walking slowly and looking around carefully. An hour later we returned to the café, having seen nothing out of the ordinary. We didn't think we would, but it was a small excuse to walk off some of our supper. Too much food as usual. We went into the café and had a coffee to discuss the next day's flying schedule.

"We know pretty well now what lies within about two hundred miles of our base," said Robert. "Let's try farther out. I suggest we take a bearing, say true north to start, and fly out about five hundred miles, then, say, ten minutes east and return. We have plenty of fuel for that. Afternoon we can reverse it and go south, then west and repeat each day."

"As good a plan as any," said George. "I'm on the base radio this week, but I'll see what else I can help with."

The next morning, we were sitting having breakfast when Bruce's mechanic, Frank, came into the kitchen. His left hand was wrapped in a bandage.

"What happened to you?" said George.

"Cut my hand on some old metal. It hurts bad, but I can still do the mapping," said Frank.

"Okay, if you want to carry on," I said, "but don't feel you have to."

"I like to help," replied Frank.

Robert, Frank, and I took off on our morning's work. Shortly after, Peter drove down to where the boat lay on the beach. George followed in our jeep with a radio.

"Can I help in any way?" asked George. "Were you going over to the other shore in the boat?"

"Not right now," said Peter. "I was just wondering if I might be able to build a big raft. I wanted to see if I could get a jeep over there. It would be an immense help. I saw some empty barrels at the junkyard the other day. It would take a raft about twelve feet wide by about twenty-five feet long. That's pretty big, but I can get the lumber needed and the barrels this afternoon."

"I'd be glad to help with the building," said George. "I'm a poor carpenter, but I can drive a nail straight at least."

"I'd welcome the help," replied Peter. "I'll get down to the lumber yard right now, then over to the junkyard. It'll probably take two or three trips."

"I can't help you with that," said George, "but I'll help you unload when you get back. I have to stay here to man the radio."

Near noon, Robert landed the plane and we all hopped in the jeep for the ride back to the farm for lunch. Bruce was on the phone, but when he finished with his conversation, he came over to our table.

"I hate to ask, but I feel I must," he said. "Can I take you up on your offer of money? I need to sell some stock as I'm short of ready cash right now and there's something we need to pay cash for."

"Sure," I said, "any time. I meant what I said. What do you need?"

"I sent my guy up to Petawawa—we heard about a couple of surplus army jeeps. He's got them, but they need to be paid for, and someone needs to drive them back. They're only a hundred dollars each, but I don't have that until I sell the stocks."

"I'll go tomorrow morning, but who can we get to drive them?" I said. "I can drive up in my car, but we'll need someone else to drive the jeeps back. Or is the army going to deliver them?"

"No, the army doesn't deliver. Albert and Bonnie have a couple of people staying with them just now. They're friends that are down and out. Maybe we can get them to help if they can drive."

Bruce got on the phone to Bonnie. The couple were asked and they both could drive and volunteered to go with me next morning.

"Will you be okay without me there tomorrow?" I asked Robert. "Is Frank capable enough at mapping?"

"He'll be fine with my coaching him; no problem that I can see," said Robert.

Peter bought thirty plastic barrels, in three loads, then a fourth load with heavy two-by-six planks and nails, from the lumber dealer.

Robert and his crew set off on their regular flight, having informed Frank of his impending duties for the morning. George helped Peter to unload and get ready to start building the raft.

"This is Don and Marg Woods," Albert said the next morning, "They're ready to help in any way they can."

"Pleased to meet you," I said. "We're going to have a long day."

"Well, we expected that," said Don. "We're prepared for it. We know what's needed, so let's get rolling."

We pulled out of the farm just after 6:00 a.m.; they were early risers. It was about a three-hour drive to Petawawa. They had eaten breakfast with Albert and Bonnie, so we drove steady until we got to the army base.

"Did Albert or Bonnie tell you what we're doing at our farm next door to their farm?"

"No," said Don, "we never seriously asked. They just said we wouldn't believe it if they told us."

"I guess that's true enough," I said. "Bonnie said you were down and out—I don't want to pry, that sort of information is private, but if you can talk about it, I may be able to help you back onto your feet. How did you get in that situation?"

"It's not a pretty story," said Don. "I was raised on a farm, and I was helping a carpenter build houses before the war, then I enlisted as soon as I was old enough. I was a private in the infantry. They didn't teach me anything except to shoot a gun. Marg and I got married before I went overseas."

"I didn't want to lose him, so we thought it would be best," said Marg.

"Anyway," continued Don, "I was too late in signing up. The war ended before I was shipped anywhere. After that, I tried to get a decent job. I had a couple of different ones but couldn't get anything permanent. The only thing left was to move back home. I don't mind the farm, but my parents want to sell and move to town. Now here I am in my thirties with a wife and no prospects. I guess we're lucky we don't have any children to complicate things."

Later that day, at the army base, we were sent straight to the quartermaster from the gate house.

"Yeah we got four jeeps here for sale," he said. "Ya aren't interested in some troop transports, are ya?"

"I might be," I said, "depending on the deal."

"Trouble is," he said, "I got too much junk hanging around here just now. What were you thinking of buying?"

"You've got some Quonset huts, as well, I'm told?"

"Lots more than I need. They're fifty bucks each, not assembled."

"All right, how about ten Quonset huts, all four jeeps and a flatbed truck, as well as a troop transport for five thousand dollars?"

"You know you're trying to rob your government?" he said, looking belligerent. "How about six hundred?"

"Now, who's trying to rob whom?" I asked, smiling. "How do I know any of this junk even works?"

"Talk to those two guys over there—they've been working on this stuff for the last two months."

Two guys who had been loitering nearby came over when he gestured toward them.

"This is Mitch Morland and Charlie Evans," he said. "They're just here to say so long—they've just been discharged."

"Hi, pleased to meet you," I said. "Is it true, as the man here says, that you've been working on these vehicles?"

"Yes, sir," said Mitch, "they're in top-notch shape."

"And he says you're heading out? I see you've got your duffel bags here. Are you going anywhere in particular?"

"We were just heading south. Ottawa or Toronto, wherever we can get jobs."

"Well, to start with I'll pay you twenty-five dollars each to drive a couple of these vehicles to Smith's Falls, just outside Ottawa. After that, maybe I can find you work and a place to stay."

"Sounds good," said Charlie. "We didn't know how we were going to get south; it would have been the bus, I guess."

"Well, are you buying this junk or what?" asked the quartermaster with a note of impatience in his voice.

"I've got to check back home," I said. "I'll let you know in a few minutes exactly what we want."

I called Bruce to explain what was available and that we could get two more men to help if he agreed. He told me to use my own judgement, as he felt I knew where we were headed with the project.

"It's sold, for five-hundred-and-fifty dollars," I said. "But we'll have to pick up the Quonset huts in a couple of days."

"You drive a hard bargain," he said. "Get it out of here as soon as you can."

We loaded two of the jeeps on the flatbed, drove to a diner and I bought the five of us lunch. When our food arrived, I said, "Do you guys know how to assemble a Quonset hut?"

"Yes, sir," said Charlie, "they taught us a lot of stuff like that. We've both been in the army since before the war."

"Would you be willing to work for me for a while?" I asked. "But you need to be able to keep things to yourselves. We're not doing anything illegal, mind you. The work is honest work."

"Jobs are scarce," said Mitch. "For a job we can be discreet."

"If you work for me, you'll see some things you will not believe. Once you've seen for yourselves what I mean, you can decide if you want to take the job. Don and Marg here are in the same boat."

"Just lead us to it," said Mitch. "We're footloose at the moment."

With Marg driving my car, Don and I driving the jeeps, and Mitch and Charlie the heavy trucks, we started the long drive back to Smith's Falls. I led the way as the others were unsure of the route.

By the time we returned, it was six o'clock. I introduced the group to Bruce, and I got out of the vehicle and Bruce opened the gate to Two Moons. We drove straight through and got out of our various vehicles.

Mitch, Charlie, Don and Marg were just standing there, their mouths agape.

"Where on earth is this?" asked Mitch.

"Well, that's just it," Bruce said, "as far as we know, *this*—as you call it—isn't on Earth. We call it Two Moons; look above you."

They were speechless, just staring around and up where both moons happened to be visible at the moment.

"Supper is over, but we have leftovers and pie for dessert," Bruce said. "If you want to come back to the farm with us, you can ask any questions you have and we'll get some beds made up for you."

Over pie and ice cream, I asked Bruce what we had in the way of large trucks to transport the Quonset huts, as well as a flatbed and a troop transport.

"We have just the one large tractor-trailer that we use to haul stuff into Two Moons," he said.

I called Mitch and Charlie over. “How many of those Quonset huts do you think we can fit onto a tractor-trailer and that stake truck we bought?”

“I’d say not more than half of what you bought. Probably less than half,” said Charlie.

“That sounds about right,” said Mitch.

“Can you two take the trucks and go pick up the remainder of the stuff tomorrow? Take as many trips as you need,” I said. “But try to get all that stuff back here in about a week.”

“Sure thing. You’re the boss,” said Mitch.

I told them I’d give them money for food and gas, and whatever else they needed.

Bruce said, “Come with me. I’ll show you where you’ll be sleeping while you’re here.”

That night, Robert, George, and I went for our patrol around town. George went west, Robert south, and I went east around the racetrack. We didn’t find anything, so we returned to the farm and went to bed.

Over breakfast, we discussed what we were going to do for the day.

“Mitch and Charlie have already set off for Petawawa,” I said. “They seem as if they’re hard workers.”

“Probably used to army life,” said George. “Do you need one of us flying with you, Robert?”

“No, that’s not necessary. Frank does a good job of mapping; that’s all we need just now. We’ll be fine by ourselves if you have something else in mind to do.”

“Peter and I could use another hand with the raft,” said George. “It’s a big job.”

"I guess that would be me," I said with a laugh. "I'm not much of a carpenter, though."

"A lot of the work is lifting and holding while someone else does the hammering," said Peter. "You'll be a welcome addition to the workforce."

Sue came by and asked, "When are the buildings going up in Two Moons? I could use a better workspace."

"We can start work on one as soon as tomorrow, if Mitch and Charlie get back today," said Bruce. "Are you starting on the inventory today?

"Yes," said Sue, "I wrote down a list of all the people we have working here yesterday. The list is getting long."

By noon, the raft was beginning to look impressive, we felt we could even finish later today. Peter was ecstatic. Two loaded transport trucks had arrived. The drivers had gone into town. Jim our home base transport driver was transferring the goods, which turned out to be a huge telescope and fittings, into Two Moons. We took time off from the ramp and unloaded the telescope into one of the caves, so that it would be protected from the elements. We didn't finish before dinner rolled around. The raft would have to wait until tomorrow.

Evening found Mitch and Charlie back with a load of metal huts.

"It's going to take at least two more trips," said Mitch. "This hardly scratches the surface"

"What did you do?" asked Bruce. "Buy out the army?"

"Well, I bought ten huts," I said. "I know we don't need them all now, but maybe we will later. Besides, I got a great deal."

We unloaded what they had brought, then went in for some coffee and dessert.

"Jim can drive the truck tomorrow or whenever you go back for the second load," said Bruce, "and then, Mitch, you can stay and we can start building one of the huts."

Peter, George, and I started work on the raft right after breakfast. Robert and Frank took off flying in a new direction. Arnie and Fred, the two shell-shocked vets from Smith's Falls whom Bruce had hired to look after the tree farm, helped Mitch start on the Quonset hut. We had the raft completed and the jeep loaded by noon. Peter would tow it to the other side with our power boat after lunch.

Arnie and Fred came over to Two Moons to volunteer their help with the Quonset hut. It turned out that they had built a few in their days in the army. They said that they loved how peaceful it was here and they had experienced a great improvement in their mental outlook.

Peter and I took some seedling trees to the far shore. Peter planned to plant some on the rolling land to the north and a few more on the open plain. George went with the crew erecting the hut. Peter and I got back by suppertime; the Quonset hut was almost complete. Jim and Mitch hadn't returned, so we went for our evening walk around town. Nothing suspicious happened. Sometime during the night, Charlie and Jim returned, very tired. There had been a road closure so they had been detoured and, thus, delayed.

The morning found us unloading yet more huts. We also found some army cots mixed in with the loads. They had obviously come from the army base, but why?

When Charlie finally woke up, we got an explanation of sorts.

"He only wanted twenty dollars for the lot of them; they were cluttering up a building using up space. I paid him out of the money we had. I hope that's all right."

"Sure, that's fine," I said. "I'm just not sure what we'll do with them."

"Mitch and I have been talking. We thought we'd like to stay here on Two Moons, if that's okay," said Charlie. "We could set up some cots in one of the huts or even sleep outdoors. We've done that often in the past."

"I'll talk to Bruce," I said, "but I don't see why not."

"We've been sleeping on the ground, as well," said Arnie. "We could use a couple of the cots."

"There are a lot more," said Charlie. "We'll bring them with tomorrow's load."

I found Bruce when we went for lunch and explained the new development with the cots.

"Sure," said Bruce. "Why not set up a sort of dormitory on Two Moons?"

I told him that Robert, George, and I had decided that we would take a week or so off. "We've got some horses running that we want to watch. Some in Toronto, some in Peterborough, and a new colt will be competing for the Gold Cup and Saucer in Prince Edward Island—we're kind of excited about that. The race is one of the big ones in PEI."

"That's not a problem on this end," he said. "You've been working hard, you deserve a holiday."

CHAPTER 6

Friday after work we jumped into our plane and flew to Peterborough. We had horses racing the next day. Robert had been doing all the flying the previous couple of weeks, so I flew us back home.

Saturday morning, we started things off with a trip to our favourite café downtown for their signature breakfast. What better way to start a small vacation? Breakfast was delicious as always; we knew what to expect.

Driving to our trainer's farm after breakfast, George said, "It's nice to be back to our old routine, even if it's just for a few days."

"I agree totally," I said. "I get a lot of pleasure from watching a horse I own run. Not just to win, but to do its best. Horses love to run."

John, Will—his driver and lead hand—and staff were still exercising horses when we pulled into the yard. Max James, Will's old friend, was standing by the practice track with a stopwatch in his hand.

"How have you been keeping, Max?" I said. "You seem to get younger every time we meet."

"I like living here with Will," he said. "It's much better than living alone on my own farm. I have people to talk to here."

John drove up with the horse he was exercising.

"We've got that gelding you bought a couple of weeks ago running for you in the seventh race," said John. "It's a conditioned race for low-class horses. The conditions are non-winners this year. This is actually his first race this year, so he has a good chance to win."

"That's what I like to hear," I said. "I like winners."

"I've got a young filly trying out her speed for the first time in the first race," said John. "It's for maidens. It looks like she'll be good, but I don't think we'll push her to win the first time out. Unless we can steal the race, of course. We also have one of our barn horses in the fifth, so it's going to be a fairly busy afternoon."

It was time for their breakfast, so we went in with them. A second cup of coffee would go down well at the moment.

"I haven't seen you three around much lately," teased Will. "I hope you're not in some sort of trouble. If the police come around, should we lie about your whereabouts?"

"We're okay," I said, "just helping a friend in Smith's Falls. He's my old roommate from university. You wouldn't want me to desert my friends, would you?"

"No, I suppose not," said Will, "particularly since we consider us to be your friends, as well."

"What time are you headed for the track?" I said.

"As soon as we're done breakfast," John said. "Get a move on, you guys."

We three, as spectators, were very early. John and staff, on the other hand, were quite late, especially since they had a runner in the first race. John's filly in the maiden race was listed as a long shot. Her name was Melanie's Hope. From hearing John talk about her, she seemed more of a sure bet than a hope, but since we didn't bet or gamble it mattered little to us. They hadn't been there long when

Will brought her out for her warm-up. The other first-race runners were also on the track. She looked as good as any of the others.

When the race started, Will took her to the front to give her a clear view of things. He meant to ease her a bit after the first half, but she had other ideas. She just kept going and started to leave the others behind. Will never urged her, and he wasn't even carrying a whip, yet she ran the race in 2:10 flat. That was an unusually good time for maidens at this track.

The barn horse's name was Warrior Will and he was owned by one of John's other owners. When Will brought him out to warm him up he was already so excited that he was totally lathered up, particularly between his back legs.

"Look at that," said Robert. "He's used up all his energy already. I wouldn't be surprised to see him finish last."

In the race itself, Will had a hard time right from the start, trying to control Warrior Will. It was all to no avail. Warrior Will broke stride at the quarter pole and he was still on a break when the rest of the racers crossed the finish line. John was going to have his work cut out for him, trying to train that out of the horse.

"I hope my gelding doesn't have that kind of problem," I said, "but he's an old campaigner. He'll probably be fine."

We went to the café for a quick coffee before the seventh.

Running Bear, my horse, looked good in the warm-up. When the race started, Will got him in at the rail at the first turn. The horses were all moving well. All of them were old campaigners, according to the program. We were laying fourth all down the backstretch, and it looked as if Will was going to be boxed in, as a horse that had been trailing started to move up on the outside. Will got him out in time as they made the clubhouse turn. We gained all the way around the turn and took the lead for good about three strides from the wire. I had a winner.

We drove out to John's after the races for a small celebration.

"You've got a great young filly there," I said. "What are your plans for her?"

"I hadn't really thought beyond getting her in this maiden race," said John, "but you're right. She won in near record time. This track is not known for being very fast."

"If I were you," I said, "I'd ship her to Toronto right now and test her against some of the best of this year's crop. You don't want to take the chance of her getting hurt here."

"You're right," said John. "She has very good breeding and she can run, that's for certain."

"We're going to Toronto now. I'll mention it to them, that you'll be bringing Melanie's Hope for some good racing. They'll be surprised at the winning speed."

Toronto on a Sunday morning was quiet. We stopped to see Leslie and the kids. Dave had already left for the track. Leslie had coffee on, expecting us.

"I'm glad you dropped in before the races," said Leslie. "I want to talk to you a little before you go."

"Is there a problem?" I asked. "Talk to me."

"It's not much of a problem, depending on how you look at it," she said. "It's really what we spoke about the last time you were here—I need a job and all the rest that goes with that."

"I remember," I replied. "I haven't forgotten. I checked around Smith's Falls. I'm not sure about opportunities around there for a veterinarian, but I know of a couple of farms that could use your services—maybe that could be a starting point."

"You've been so good to our family and helping me get my diploma; we don't want to upset you by moving away and leaving you high and dry. We've been looking after your houses to help us with food and rent for a while now."

"You don't have to worry about any of that. I can get someone else to look after my property. I'm just not sure what kind of work I can find for Dave."

"Dave and I have talked about it. We don't want our kids growing up in the city. We want to get back to the country. We've put aside a little money. Maybe someday we can get a place of our own, but Dave can work at anything. He's very handy."

"Well, maybe we can solve all that, but I can't say just now. Why don't you come down to Smith's Falls and we'll see where it goes from there? When would you be ready to go?"

"Dave has already given his notice. We were going to move to Bobcaygeon or Fenelon Falls, but Smith's Falls sounds okay, if there are some prospects there. We don't know of anything available around here."

"Good, then it's settled; come to Smith's Falls. We'll be there by next Monday, so any time after that. I'll give you the phone number."

The track in Toronto had a good dining room so we went there for lunch. Our Toronto trainer was there, eating lunch by himself, and invited us to sit with him.

"Dave has quit," he said. "He wants to move out of Toronto. I have a new guy set to go, so it's no problem. Thanks for lending him to me for the past four years."

"I hope he did well for you," I said. "Leslie told us, and we sort of expected the move."

"He was a good guy to work with," he said. "I wish him well. I just have the one horse of yours now and he's running today. I guess that's why you're here. Dorset Lightning has been a good horse and quite consistent but he's getting old. I'll be sorry to see him retire in a year or two."

"John has a new filly that he's shipping to you. You'll probably have her this week. She won a maiden in Peterborough in two minutes ten seconds."

"That's fast! I'll be happy to get her. There are some really good filly races coming up soon. We'll see what she can do for time on a faster track here. The mile track here should show her best stuff, but if she can do two-ten there on a half-mile track, she'll be very competitive here"

The very first race produced a long delay. One of the horses broke stride late. The driver gave the horse a couple of strokes with the whip. The horse didn't like that and tried to jump the inner fence to get away from the whip. The horse ended up breaking one of its front legs and had to be put down. I didn't like to see that, so we went into the clubhouse for coffee while order was restored.

Dorset Lightning was in the sixth race. He started out well, at the rail in second place. Unfortunately, that was the closest he got to the front. I guess he needed to be dropped down a couple of classes; he had done his best, but his best was not good enough for that class. I had made a lot of money from the purses he had won over the years. He didn't have to retire just yet. But when it came time, John would supply him with a good home at his farm.

We were flying out to Prince Edward Island in the morning. Leslie had made supper for us: mashed potatoes, roast beef, gravy, cauliflower, beans, and turnips. With apple pie for dessert. The roast beef was great. Seasoned just right and falling apart, it was so tender—almost as good as the Two Moons roast we had at Bruce's.

"If we're late getting back from Prince Edward Island, do you have enough money to stay at a motel in Smith's Falls until we return?" I asked Dave.

"You don't have to look out for us anymore," said Dave, "we're all grown up. We'll be fine."

Morning found us in the sky again, headed for Prince Edward Island. We hadn't seen our friends there in nearly a year.

"You know," Robert said, "you did a good job getting those Quonset huts but it's too bad we couldn't get one of those bigger ones like we had during the war. We could have used it to hangar the plane on Two Moons. It's out in the open now and gets rained on every day. It would last longer if we could hangar it."

"That's a good idea," I replied. "I'll see what we can do when we get back to Smith's Falls."

Randy picked us up at the Charlottetown airport and drove us to his farm near Crapaud. We went at once to see the young colt, the apple of Randy's eye.

"He'll win the Cup and Saucer." Randy beamed. "He's the fastest colt I've ever trained."

"That's what we're here to witness," said George. "The big race is only two days away. Do you have something planned for tomorrow?"

"Yes, sir," said Randy. "I've got a boat all lined up for some deep-sea fishing, namely mackerel. They're running heavy this year. You're in for some good fun!"

We got the boat out of Rustico Harbour at 7:00 a.m. The gulf was as calm as I'd ever seen it. A good thing it was, as George tended to get seasick very easy. We only went about a mile out before slowing down to get to fishing. Our captain for the day was Dominic Gallant.

I said, "Gallant is a pretty common Island name, but Dominic is unusual. How did you come by that as a given name?"

"My mother's parents came from Italy a long time ago," he replied. "They set up a restaurant in Charlottetown. My mother liked the name, nothing fancy."

Randy brought over a roll of tin foil. "You don't need any fancy lures for Mackerel," he said. "Just tie a little scrap of this near the bare hook. They'll even hit a bare hook, but this is better."

Randy had five fishhooks all on one line about three or four feet apart. We waited about ten minutes with nothing happening, then Randy yelled, "Here they come." Suddenly, we all had fish on at the same time. Chaos reigned. Randy had fish on three of the hooks. They were all swimming in different directions, or at least trying to. We got them all in and just threw the bait back out. It seemed only seconds and we had more fish on hooks. After about a half hour that seemed like forever, the school swam away. We had filled a barrel with our catches. We sat down for a rest and Dominic brought us coffees.

"We'll just have a small break and see if we can find another school," said Dominic. "Then we've got roast beef for lunch. Cooked by my wife but we'll reheat it on the camp stove and have a nice baked potato with it. There are carrots, as well."

The roast beef turned out to be some of the best I had ever eaten. Dominic said afterward that it was just the sea air. We all stuffed ourselves anyway.

Gold Cup and Saucer day started out in an anticlimactic fashion; it was, however, a big day in the lives of many Prince Edward Islanders. We skipped the parade altogether and went straight to the track. It was very festive there with the midway and all the activities going on, but we had slept in, so the races were about to start by the time we arrived.

Randy joined us after a while. He had left his men in charge of the colt. He had hired the best driver he could get.

"I told my driver to just take him to the front and see if he could stay there," he said. "I've heard that some of the regular drivers here don't want us to win. They think that Ocean Ann should not be counted as an Island horse and that our colt should not be running. My guys will keep him safe until race time. We need to avoid any dirty tricks they've got planned."

"You seem to attract that type of trouble," I exclaimed. "But you're an Islander yourself! I don't understand the ill will toward you."

"There is a small inner circle of owners and drivers at the track here," said Randy. "They like to control what is happening. They don't like anyone else butting in."

"Well, good luck with him," I said. "It sounds as if you know what you're up against. That sort of prejudice happens elsewhere, as well."

Very soon it was time for the race. The horses came out for the parade and then lined up. Ocean Sunshine went straight for the lead as Randy had said he would. He was four lengths ahead at the quarter pole. The other drivers must have caught on to what was happening, because they started making individual runs at him. One horse would put on a burst of speed to catch up, then that horse would drop back and another horse would do the same.

"Look," said Randy, "they're trying to wear him out by making him run faster to stay ahead."

"Don't worry so much," I said, "it might be working a wee bit but, your driver has only shaken the reins at him, so far, to keep his distance. He's well within himself by what I see."

"They just passed the three-quarter mark. I think that's the fastest ever for a three quarter at this track," said Randy.

The race finished with Ocean Sunrise well clear of the pack.

"Look at that!" exclaimed Randy. "That's only two ticks off the track record, and he wasn't even pushed."

"I think you should send him up to the Big Smoke," I said. "He needs to be tried against the best two-year-olds in the country. There are big dollars available for horses that can run like that."

"Can you help me arrange that?" Randy asked. "I'd like to see how he can do against the best."

"I'd be proud to do that for you," I said. "I have a trainer in Toronto that's one of the best available. He'd be glad to have him."

CHAPTER 7

I picked up Dave and Leslie and their kids Monday afternoon. When we got to the farm, I took them straight through to Two Moons, having obtained permission from Bruce. They were totally amazed and incredulous. I explained that we had two operating farms here on Two Moons and what Bruce and his friends had found out about this planet and what they were doing.

"The first farm was set up five years ago with five dairy cattle and a bull. That has now increased to about fifty milking cows. The second farm was set up about the same time, but that family liked pigs. They started with five Tamworth sows and a boar. They were talked into adding a beef herd two years ago. Both farms have some chickens. The second farm supplies all of our bacon."

"I'd like to get back into farming," said Dave. "Maybe here would be a good place. Do you need another farm on Two Moons? This is good-looking land. Is it all covered with this short grass.? How do the cattle respond to it?"

"They seem to take to it very well," I said. "I'm not sure about all the ins and outs, but you can talk to the two couples who are already here. I don't really know whether Bruce is in favour of adding more farms," I added. "I'll ask. Maybe you could take over the beef operation. Both farms grow their own grain crops for feed. You may be better off starting a farm on the Earth side. I just showed you this as I wanted to show Leslie where a vet is needed. We could round up some herds back outside for you to look after."

"I'm anxious to start farming on my own but we haven't enough money, and I have a feeling this place will grow," said Dave. "I'd like to be in on it. How could I arrange to buy here instead?"

"Why don't we go eat and we'll see what can be arranged," I said.

At supper I introduced the Gransdens to Bruce and asked him about the possibility of adding another farm on Two Moons.

"Well, Jordan and Mae Fountain are not really beef people. I know they would love to unload that part of the operation on somebody else," said Bruce. "Would you like to take over that part?" he asked Dave. "We also need to start a market garden farm. Is that something you would be interested in?"

"Beef cattle is what I know best," said Dave. "I know a little about market gardens, and I would be willing to give it a go. How much do you want for the land and what arrangements can I make to pay for it?"

"First of all," said Bruce, "there is no need to pay for the land, but you'll have to string fences and a lot of other things to get started. It's just bare, raw land. It would be best if you worked with Ron, here, to get you set up. It's going to be a lot of hard work."

"We don't mind hard work," said Dave, "but surely this is too good to be true? We'll also need machinery and we don't have the money to pay for that," said Dave.

"Don't worry about that," I said. "I'll loan you the money for the equipment, and you can pay me back slowly out of what you produce. There's a big farm machinery manufacturer right here in Smith's Falls. We'll go down there soon and get you what you need."

The next morning found us back on Two Moons. Dave, Leslie and I gathered with George, Robert and Frank at the plane.

"Robert, George and Frank have been mapping this world. Robert and George, you've met the Gransdens before, and this here is Bruce's airplane mechanic, Frank. We've had some problems around Smith's Falls lately. Frank's cousin was raped and murdered, and then the same thing happened to another girl. We've been helping out by doing some late-night patrols, seeing if we come across anything suspicious, but so far we've come up empty-handed. George is a retired police officer, so he knows what to be on the lookout for."

"I've been thinking about the case a lot and I feel as if there's something I just can't quite put my finger on," said George. "It'll come to me—it always does."

"Today, Frank is going up with Robert, so George and I will see if we can set you up with some decent land," I said. "I think the better land is actually on the other shore, so we'll take a jeep across. We can leave the kids here to be babysat while we look around. We have a raft that will hold the jeep. The raft was Peter's idea—he's our plant specialist. If you get into the market garden side of things, you'll find him handy to have around. Let's say we start you off with a mile-by-a-mile. You probably don't want to fence all that at once, but we'll be able to see where to put a house. We only have seven beef cattle here at the moment, and a couple of steers, but we can get a bull and maybe a few more cattle."

"This is all completely overwhelming," said Leslie. "Thank you. You've always been too good to us."

Leslie got in the boat with me. Dave and George got on the raft with the jeep, for us to tow it across the river.

"A couple of acres are enough to get a fence around for that many cows. Maybe later we can get some more fencing," said Dave. "Do you know where we can get some?"

"Oh, you won't need that—Bruce bought up a bankrupt company that had tonnes of fencing. You'll find all you need in a cave in those small mountains to the east there," I told him. "You just have to decide where you want to set up. We can help some and there are some other people around here who'll help, too."

"This looks like a good spot," said Dave as we drove along. "Hey, those young trees over there look like oak and maple, and maybe some pines."

"Peter just planted those a couple of weeks ago. They're just seedlings, but they'll grow fast here."

"Which way does the weather come from?" asked Dave. "You've been here a while . . . Do you know?"

"It sweeps down this way," I said. "There hasn't been much in the way of precipitation, but it does rain. Bruce says we're in a temperate zone here. No drastic weather of any kind. Winter and summer are not too different. You can grow a couple of crops per year. The gravity seems lighter though."

"This spot here seems as good as any," said Dave. "What do you think, Les?"

"It looks good to me," Leslie said. "We could build over there and when the trees grow it will be sheltered."

"Great," said Dave. "We can fence off about ten acres or so as a start. All we need is the wire. Tomorrow maybe we can go into town and see what we can do about a house."

"We'll have to see about a bank loan at the same time to finance it," said Leslie. "We have enough for a small house if we don't have to pay for the land, but if we're going to be staying here we'll need something bigger, eventually. Our family is growing."

"Don't worry about that," I said. "I'll pay for it and you can pay me back when you can. Buy something big enough for all eventualities. Beaver Lumber is probably best—they have house designs and the lumber to do it."

"Let's go and see this wire," said Dave. "We're going to need to get a fence up if we're getting cattle any time soon."

"Hop in the jeep," I told him. "We need to get back to the other shore. After we look at the wire, we'll have lunch, then you can take the jeep back here and explore around. There don't appear to be any wild animals over on this side, so you should be safe."

"You've got enough wire here to fence in a good-sized planet," said Dave. "What are you going to do with it all?"

"Bruce isn't sure what to do with it," I said, "but we'll find a use. Let's go have some lunch. All the food at Bruce's is grown on Two Moons. A small portion of it gets marketed, but the majority is used to feed ourselves."

Entering the main house, we met Sue. "This is Sue McGregor," I said to Dave and Leslie. "She's Bruce's assistant. Sue is taking an inventory of all the people we've got working here and all the goods we have on hand just now. If you need anything, just ask. If we don't have it, Sue'll find it for you."

"Pleased to meet you," said Sue. "Is there anything you need?"

"Not that I can think of at the moment," said Dave.

"Let me see if I can get you some help to string the fence," I said.

I brought over Arnie and Fred and introduced them to Dave and Leslie. "They look after the forest that we've planted on Two Moons. They also have experience stringing wire."

While we were talking, Don and Marg Woods came over. "We used to own a farm," Don said. "We'll help, as well. We're going to take over the orchard part of the woods that Arnie and Fred presently work on. The trees in the orchard are starting to produce a lot of fruit. We've got several acres of berry bushes, too."

"That would be great," said Dave. "I can use the help. Then we can start raising beef sooner. Maybe we can buy some fruit trees to harvest ourselves."

We spent the rest of the day bringing the wire back to their lot. The work crew vowed to get started on the stringing of the fence tomorrow.

Robert returned near the end of the day. "I need Peter for tomorrow," he said. "We found some vegetation. It doesn't look like much, maybe something similar to bamboo. Peter will know what to call it. I see that the builders have finished the first of the Quonset huts. I don't think it's big enough to store the airplane, though."

"We'll check out the size tomorrow, but I bet you're right,'" I said. "When you're out with Peter tomorrow, I'll see what we can get as an alternative. The builder crew are starting on another Quonset hut tomorrow. We'll have two done by the end of the week."

"We're getting quite a nice little community started here," said George. "What are we going to do with it all?"

"I guess that would be up to Bruce," I said. "Let's get ready for our patrol around Smith's Falls tonight," I said. "I'd like to catch this monster."

"We'll have to get lucky," said George, "but sometimes luck happens."

We went out and did our walk around Smith's Falls as usual. We came back with the same results: not a single clue. Luck wasn't on our side tonight.

At breakfast, Robert said to Bruce, "Those fish you seeded the lake with four or five years ago, did they live?"

"Oh, yes," said Bruce, "they've grown up quite nicely. Were you thinking of trying to fish for them?"

"I think it might be good recreation for the weekend," replied Robert.

"Sounds like a good idea to me," said Bruce, "but let our resident brains test them before you eat them."

"Sure," said Robert, "it should be fun, anyway."

"I heard a good joke the other day," said George

"George is our group's funny guy," I said.

George started. "It was entertainment night at the seniors' centre and the Amazing Claude was topping the bill. People came from miles around to see the famed hypnotist do his stuff. As Claude went to the front of the meeting room, he announced, 'Unlike most hypnotists who invite two or three people up here to be put into a trance, I intend to hypnotize each and every member of the audience.'

"The excitement was almost electric as Claude withdrew a beautiful antique pocket watch from his coat. 'I want you each to keep your eye on this antique watch. It's a very special watch. It's been in my family for six generations.' He began to swing the watch gently back and forth while quietly chanting, 'Watch the watch, watch the watch, watch the watch . . .'

"The crowd became mesmerized as the watch swayed back and forth, light gleaming off its polished surface. Hundreds of pairs of eyes followed the swaying watch, until, suddenly, it slipped from the hypnotist's fingers and fell to the floor, breaking into a hundred pieces.

"'SH**!' said the hypnotist. 'It took three days to clean up the seniors' centre!'"

Everybody had a good laugh.

Robert took off with Frank and Peter to see the vegetation that had been found the previous day. George and I headed to town to see if we could track down a building that we could use as a hangar. We went to the lumber yard.

"We're looking to set up a small barn or similar type of structure and we wondered if you could help us with some suggestions," I said to the clerk.

"Certainly. We have everything you need," said the clerk. "How big of a building did you have in mind?"

"I'm not sure," I said, "but big enough to hold a large quantity of hay."

"We have plans here for several different sizes," the clerk said. "We can get the rafters pre-made and supply all the lumber. How much did you plan on spending?"

"I'm not sure," I said. "What sort of range do you have?"

"It so happens that I can offer you a really good price on a mid-size barn. A farmer ordered one a while ago and we had it shipped it to his place then found out he couldn't pay for it, so it's being returned today."

"How much would you take for it?" I said. "And how much was it originally?"

"Well, we don't really want it back, so I'll give it to you for just over the half-price mark. But you'll have to take it now."

"Do we get the set of plans with it?" I said

"Yes, all you need to do is pour the concrete floor the right size and you're off to the races."

"Okay," I said, "you've got a deal. I'll write you a cheque. You can deliver it out to the farm anytime."

"It'll be there this afternoon. It's still on the truck, so I'll send it right out."

"That worked out pretty well," I said to George, once we got back in the truck. "He gave us a really good price. Let's ask Jim to get some more cement and we'll get the rest of the work force to build a mould for it. If we all get at the framing for the cement, we might be able to start to pour it tomorrow, or at worst, the next day."

"We got more than half of the fence up this morning," said Dave, once we got back to Two Moons. "These guys work fast and know what they're doing with fence wire. We'll be done tomorrow morning for certain."

"Great! We need to get the framing for the big shed started as soon as we can," I told him. "I'd like to get the work force going on the barn tomorrow."

"We can handle that task, as well," said Arnie. "All we need to know is the size. We'll get the concrete poured over the weekend. With the right weather, which we usually have, it should take about three days to cure. Then we can start to build. When do we get the lumber?"

"It should already be in the yard. Jim can start bringing it in anytime."

"Peter brought a lot of little shoots back in pots this morning," said Robert. "We're going back for more this afternoon."

"Dave," said Peter, "do you mind if we plant some on your land, or that side of the river at any rate? They could be a good source of income in the future. I'd like to try some over there without using fertilizer and some on this side using manure and see which grows better."

"That sounds like a good plan," said Dave. "I think we'll have the fence finished this afternoon, so I can go get the cattle tomorrow morning. This place is great!"

After lunch, Peter and Robert took off to get more plants. George and I drove out to the Smith's Falls airport to grab our fishing gear from the plane. When we got back, we started getting the lumber organized for the barn. Everybody was working hard.

"What kind of fish should we try for?" I said to George over dinner. "I'd like to try for bass first, then maybe pickerel next week. They stocked a lot of game fish, as well as food fish for the game fish to eat. If they survived, they should be well grown. That was five years ago."

"That sounds like a good idea," said George. "Also the hangar or barn, or whatever it's going to be called, looks on track to be set up for next week. This colony is getting bigger by the day."

It had been a busy day, but we went into town around ten o'clock to do a patrol. We found nothing, but we decided to keep at it. It wasn't likely that the rapist had just given up.

CHAPTER 8

Dave and Leslie had just sat down for dinner when I walked into the dining room on Friday evening. "How is the fencing going?" I asked

"We completed about twenty acres this morning, so I spent the afternoon helping with the barn that you're putting up for a hangar. We completed the frame for the floor concrete. Jim will be pouring all weekend. It will probably need about three days to cure, then we can start building. Speaking of that, Leslie and I are going into town tomorrow morning. We're going to the lumber yard first to order lumber for our house."

"I didn't know that you had a house plan in mind," I said.

"Bruce showed us several house plans that he had, complete with blueprints. One of the plans, he used for the houses he has here on the Earth side for his guests, but he had others. We picked out a sort of a ranch style with one side open and rooms around a central court. Kitchen and dining room on one side, living room in the middle and bedrooms along the other side. Washroom and furnace rooms in the corners. We're going to put a swimming pool in the courtyard. We have enough money for that. You did say we could borrow the money from you to buy the farm equipment?" asked Leslie.

"Yes," I said, "and I meant it. I don't want you to just buy the minimum. I will be angry with you if you try that. I want you to get everything you think you might need. Go to that farm equipment manufacturer in town. When you get everything set, tell him I'll be in the next day to pay him."

"We've said many times that you are too good to us, but we're going to take full advantage of this opportunity."

"If you don't, I'll be after you," I said. "I want your farm to do well. Buy all the equipment you need for planting as well as farming, and even to help with construction. And I want Leslie to be successful as a vet, too."

Saturday, Robert, George, and I got in the power boat and took it up to the falls. We had decided if we were the fish, that might be a place we would hang out. We had decided to use artificial lures for our first attempt. George was the first to be ready as we pulled to a stop and put the anchor down. He had a hit on his second cast and wound in a two-pound bass. While he was getting his hook out, I made a cast and ended up with an almost identical fish.

"Well, we know the fish are here and are biting," said Robert, who had caught a fish of his own on by that time. He had only made three casts. "Let's keep two for the chemist to analyze and release all the others."

"Sounds good," I said. "We know the fish are here, at least. Let's try farther down the river." We pulled up the anchor and moved about a mile downstream. It took four or five casts but we each caught one by about the fifth or sixth cast. Mine was a pickerel.

"I guess we've answered the question of the fish surviving," I said. "They appear to be here in spades. Since we won't be eating any just yet, let's go back, give these two fish to the chemistry people and see if we can help with the building effort."

By lunchtime, Dave and Leslie had returned from their shopping trip. They were quite excited. "We spent a lot of your money," said Leslie a bit sheepishly. "We probably got a lot of stuff we won't use very often, but we'll need to plant crops for food for the cattle."

"That's great!" I said. "I'll go in this afternoon and square up. They can start to deliver Monday morning. You'll need to be here so you can drive it to your place on Two Moons. How did it go at the lumber yard?"

"They didn't have everything we need for the house, but they promised it all within a week," said Dave. "We even rented a small portable cement mixer for later in the week. I got a small shovel attachment for the tractor. With that, I can do my own excavating for the house as well as the swimming pool. Later I can do excavation work for other people."

"Good to see that you're thinking ahead," I said. "I like that."

After church on Sunday, we took the boat and trailered it up to the lake above the falls.

"I liked the sermon today," I told George, who had stayed back to help the work crew while I went to church in the morning. "The quotes were taken from John 11, verses 17 to 44. It's the story of Lazarus and his resurrection. Jesus is talking to Martha. He says, 'Your brother will rise again.'

"She replies, 'I know he will rise again in the resurrection at the last day.' Then He says to her, 'I am the resurrection and the life. Those who believe in me will live, even if they die; Martha do you believe this?'

"To me that means God is all powerful and can do anything. I take that to mean He can reincarnate, as well as resurrect. So, maybe if God wills it, he will also reincarnate those who want to be reincarnated."

"That's not quite the way most churches look at that passage," said George, "but who knows what the original Greek or Aramaic actually said?"

When Monday arrived, we set up for George to fly the mapping trips with Robert. Nearly everyone else was working on the hangar. I was manning the radio, in touch with the flyers. After the first hour, I got an SOS from the plane. They had made an emergency landing. The engine had stopped. They were almost at the end of the outward leg, near where they would be turning around to do the return leg; a long way from home with no food. They were okay, though; Robert had made many open-field landings during the war. He radioed back shortly to say that they had no gas even though the gauge was reading full still. The good part was we had some reasonable maps we could use to get some gas to them. Nobody had ever been that far away from the compound before. We set up a schedule to talk with them, in order to conserve the plane's batteries, and I started rounding up the essentials to take to them. I figured it would take us two or three days to get there. They had water but little else.

First thing, we went to the airport in Smith's Falls and got a direction finder. Sue gathered enough food for everyone. We had two walkie-talkies, but we could have used more. I asked Bruce if he could track down a couple more at a surplus store while we were gone. We decided to take the big troop transport and a jeep. The troop transport would carry lots of gas in cans, as well as lumber and anything else that we considered necessary to get across the rivers and any other obstacle we might find in between.

As soon as we got organized, we were off, headed east. It was late afternoon. First, we had to get around the small mountain range. We got around the mountain range late in the evening, so we stopped to camp for the night. We were exhausted. Before we went to bed, we took a triangulation on the plane. It showed that they were 270 miles from base camp, and that we were still about 270 miles from them, an almost equilateral triangle. The night was quite bright, with both moons in the sky.

Early morning found us back on the way to rescue the stranded flyers. The first of the obstacles we faced for the day was a river that was too deep for us at the point we encountered it. The troop transport went south, while we, in the jeep, went north to see if we could find a shallow place to cross. We found it first: a widening and, thus, much shallower point in the river. We called the transport on our walkie-talkie, and they came north. We crossed one at a time in case we got stuck in a soft spot. The crossing had cost us a couple of hours.

Almost at once we came to another river. This one was not as wide nor as deep. The transport went first and got across. When we tried with the jeep, it stalled in the middle of the river and we had to use the winch on the transport to haul us out. We drove for nearly 70 miles before encountering another river. These were by far the biggest problems.

We added to our maps by finding an extinct volcano—a huge one—and several more patches of the bamboo. One was very large, a veritable forest. In another spot we found a giant crater in the ground. It looked as if it had been hit by a meteor.

The ground we found to be mostly level but with some gentle slopes. This made travelling easier, but the miles we were travelling were not a straight line. We stopped a couple of times. At the designated hour, we made contact with Robert and George. The batteries on the plane were getting weak on our last contact, so I suggested skipping a couple of contact times. This would save the batteries a little. We fought our way over another river and since it was late, we stopped and camped.

Next morning, we tried to talk to Robert and George but got nothing. We had to guess that the plane batteries had given out. They had also had nothing to eat for two days now. Luckily, they had water. It was getting more urgent to keep moving. According to our map we were only about 70 miles from them. We had three more rivers to cross, according to the map we had. The map was getting a lot more detailed as we went.

Late afternoon we reached them.

"Boy, are we happy to see you guys," said George. "Where is the food? We're starved!"

"We're completely out of gas," said Robert. "I usually put a dipstick in the tank, but I must have just looked at the needle on the meter. I can't believe I did that after all these years I've been flying."

"Are you guys okay otherwise?" I asked. "You look fine."

They said they were. We used our generator to recharge the plane's batteries. Then we refilled the gas tanks. The gas gauge said it was full the whole time. Robert and George got in. The plane started with no trouble. They took off for home, and we started our return trip. This trip took a lot less time than the trip out as we now knew where the portages were. Very little good had come out of this catastrophe. But we had at least learned where there was more bamboo and we were able to add to our maps.

We now knew we should have two airplanes here. Perhaps more generators would be beneficial, as well. Our power had been stretched to the limit.

We drove into the home compound at last. We could see things had been happening. There were a couple of newly built picnic tables. Everybody was there to greet us.

"What's going on?" I asked Robert.

"We're celebrating our rescue!" said Robert. "Go get cleaned up so we can get things rolling. Bruce purchased a whole truckload of lobster fresh from the east coast. The guy just arrived in town, and Bruce saw him and the idea was born. They've baked cakes and pies and cookies. You name it, we got it."

"I like a party," I said. "I'll just run in and get changed and have a shave and shower." When I returned half an hour later, Bruce yelled, "Now that all the rescuers are here, let's start the celebration!"

I had never seen so many people gathered on Two Moons before; I counted 29 people in all. "Where did all these people come from?" I asked Bruce. "There are people here I've never even met."

"Albert and Bonnie Black are here from next door, but otherwise it's just our people," said Bruce. "Most of these people are usually just really busy working away in different parts of the compound."

"The food looks great," I said, "and I'm starving! Let's go get some." I started to head toward the buffet table.

"Oh no, you don't. You were part of the rescue crew," said Bruce, steering me toward a table. "We've got special service for the rescuers. Take a seat and someone will get your order."

At a wave from Bruce, Leslie Gransden came walking over. "What will you have?" she asked.

Smiling at her, I said, "I understand there is lobster. I'll have a serving of lobster with some potato and veggies."

"There is enough lobster for at least one each, plus a second, if you want another. What kind of potatoes would you like? We have scalloped, baked, mashed or roasted."

"I'll have a baked potato with lots of butter, and some veggies," I replied.

"Do you want all the kinds of veggies? We have green beans, carrots, cauliflower, broccoli, spinach, turnip and squash."

"Cauliflower, carrots and beans will be plenty," I said.

"Would you like a roll and a green salad, as well? The rolls are freshly baked."

"Yes, I'll have a salad and roll. Just tell me how I'm supposed to eat all this!"

"Just do the best you can," she said, grinning, "Think of it as an all-you-can-eat-buffet. There is steak, as well, for those who don't like lobster."

Dave came over to my bench and sat down with his heaped plate.

"There's so much food," I said, shaking my head in disbelief.

"The cooks have been at it since last night," said Dave, laughing. "Just wait until you see all the desserts."

"That's incredible," I said. "I don't think I'll have room after the main course, though."

"You better find room," he said. "If you don't at least try some, you'll be insulting the cooks."

My food arrived via Leslie and Bonnie Black. It looked delicious. I said a brief prayer and dug in.

"How's the farm coming?" I asked Dave when my mouth was clear. "Has the machinery arrived and have you been able to get it over the river to the farm?"

"I'm only missing one piece," said Dave. "That's due later today. We found a shallow place in the river about two miles south of where we're going to build. The river widens out at one point and it's easy to cross. We got some hens from one of the other farms and I was able to build a coop in between helping to build the hangar. We'll get some feed crops for the cattle in as soon as next week. I'm eager to get things rolling."

"I always knew you were a go-getter," I said. "Congratulations. Have you got the cattle over yet?"

"Yes, we drove them over two days ago and installed them in their pasture. I have seven cows and a bull. After I get more fence up, I want to buy another breed of beef cattle and another bull, but that'll have to wait for a while. There are too many other things to do."

Leslie came over to get my dessert order and I looked down at my plate, surprised to discover it was empty.

"Would you like another lobster or any other first course item?" she asked, "or are you ready for some dessert?"

"That's all for me," I said. "Thanks, anyway."

"You don't dare quit now. The cooks, including me, will beat you to a pulp and sit on you!"

"Okay, okay," I said, "maybe something small. What have you got?"

"We have, peaches, pears, apples, two kinds of cherries and two kinds of plums. We have apple pies, lemon pies, plum pies, peach pies, and cherry pies. Cakes are chocolate with chocolate icing, vanilla, carrot or peach—with ice cream, of course. I probably forgot something . . ."

"I protest!" I said. "How can I be expected to choose from all that?"

She just smiled at me, tapping her foot.

"Well, I suppose I could eat a small piece of chocolate cake with chocolate frosting and a small slice of peach pie."

"That's okay for a start," she said with a wink, and disappeared in the direction of the trestle table were the food was set up.

"Don't be too hard on them," said Dave. "They just want to show you that you are appreciated and well liked."

"Yes, I understand," I replied. "But getting our friends back wasn't all that much."

"Everybody else thinks so," said Dave. "We want you, Robert and George to come down to our place for dinner as soon as possible. We also want to show you our appreciation."

"I'd love that," I said. "Have you talked to Robert and George about it yet?"

"Yes, they're all for it, but I think Robert has a fly-by in Ottawa next week with his Spitfire. It's Canada Day. Albert and Bonnie would like you to go to Belleville Tuesday to watch their horse race there"

"I'd like to get back to Peterborough for a couple of days, as well, to see how my horses are doing, so how about in two weeks we come for supper?"

"Sounds good," Dave said.

Bruce came wandering by. "Great party," he said. "I like lots of good food. We'll be eating leftovers for a week, I'm sure."

"Have you talked to Robert and George today?" I asked.

"Yes," he said, "from what I hear, you three are taking off for a week to do some racing."

"Does that pose any sort of problem?"

"Not at all. I've got some high-powered mathematicians coming to discuss the phenomenon we have here, so I'm going to be plenty busy with them."

CHAPTER 9

The party finally wound down. Too late after the fact, we realized that we could have trailered our plane, which was sitting out at the Smith's Falls airport. It would probably have taken a day to get it to the farm, but that would have shortened the rescue by about a day, maybe more. Sometimes a person doesn't see the solution to a problem until it has already been solved by other means.

"Robert," I said, "I think we need another aircraft here at Two Moons. I don't expect another crisis, but one never knows."

"That would be good," he said. "I saw an advertisement for some old DC3s in a magazine. They've been sitting idle since the war but have been taken care of by mechanics. They should be cheap. Didn't you spend some time flying them during the war?"

"Indeed, I did," I said. "Just a few hours, but I think the idea has merit. I'll look into it next week. This week I'd like to concentrate on our horses and some recreation. We've been working hard."

Bruce came over to say, "I've decided to get more generators. At least one big one and several more portable ones. Our little community on Two Moons has been growing rapidly. The need is there already, but I intend to officially announce the discovery to the world. They didn't believe me last time, but I think they will when we have our community to show."

"When do you plan to do this?" I asked.

"Oh, maybe around Labour Day or just a bit afterward," he said. "I'm going to sell off plots of land if I can. I don't know if I can lay claim to all of Two Moons, but I can't see how anyone can complain. We've put a lot into it. You fellows will be in for a share. We'll talk about that later."

"It's a great place," I said. "I think I'd like to settle here later. We'll see how it goes. We're off to Belleville today to cheer on Bonnie and Albert in their race there. We'll see you in about a week."

On Tuesday, we met Albert and Bonnie as they drove up to the track in Belleville.

"Nice little track here," I said. "The purses are quite small, though. You should have brought him to Peterborough. He'd have had a better chance of earning a few dollars."

"That's too far away," said Albert. "This is closer. I like to have a winner now and then, so we come here. The money won is not that important."

"Peterborough isn't that much farther," I said. "I bet we could get you in at a class where you would have a good chance of winning. We have a good presence there and our trainer is well respected. You could stable him at John's farm and stay with one of us. It would cost you a lot less overall."

"I see what you mean. Next time we should do that. What do you think, Bonnie?"

"I like the idea," said Bonnie.

"Have you considered how you're going to drive the race?" asked George.

"I thought that I'd just to come out at a nice even pace at the start, then pull out when I start up the backstretch the second time and stay on the outside from then until the wire. This is a half-mile track, which is what he's used to. The race is a little longer that way, but it saves his energy until the end. He can do a pretty good quarter when you ask him."

"Sounds like a good strategy," said George. "I wish you luck."

The race started just as Albert had said, with his horse, Broadway Jack, in third place at the rail. There were six horses total in the race. That left him a good chance to win part of the purse at least. Albert pulled Broadway Jack to the outside and accelerated. He came up rapidly gaining. He was even with the leading horse as they swept around the final turn, pulling away as he came down the stretch to win by an easy length. Bonnie was jumping up and down and ran down to the winner's circle for the winning picture.

After the race, we all gathered at a restaurant that Bonnie recommended for a victory supper. They headed home afterward, and we went on to Toronto.

"A great start to the week," commented Robert. "Maybe the luck thing will follow us home."

"Let's hope for that to happen," I said. "Last week our luck was mostly bad."

"Oh, I wouldn't say that," said George. "We were rescued and that's good."

The house that Dave and Leslie had rented from me while living in Toronto was still vacant. That was not a big problem as I owned eight other houses and a small apartment building, and those units were all still rented. Money was still coming in to help pay for my Smith's Falls expenditures. We stayed at a hotel near the track. Our Toronto trainer, Bert Mason, met us for breakfast. "I got your message that you were coming. I don't have anything for you just now. That colt, High Society, you bought when you were here last is training well. Just when he'll make it to the track is uncertain yet, but so far so good," he said.

"We just came to see if there were any other horses we could pick up," I said, "either through claimers, or a straight sale. We need some for racing here and in Peterborough."

"A lot of good colts are starting to come down in price, now that their trainers are seeing that they're not good enough for the big-time-stakes races. There's a colt that is racing in a claimer for the first time today—he'd cost about a $100,000, though. Do you want to go that high?"

"If you think he's worth the money," I said, "then let's get him."

"He's well worth it in my opinion. I think he's just a late bloomer," he said. "There should be a few other cheaper claimers available through private sales, as trainers start to unload stock that they can't use any longer."

"We'd like to get two or three to race in Peterborough. Can you set up a couple of good ones for us?"

"You bet. I can think of at least three, maybe four, right off the start. We could see them today if you like. If we make deals for them, I can make arrangements with John to get them shipped up to his barn."

"We've finished breakfast. Can we get started right away?" I asked.

"You guys sit here and have another cup of coffee," he replied. "I'll slip over to the track. It's not far and I'll put in a claim for the colt. It'll only take a couple of minutes. Then we can go shopping. Let's hope nobody else already has a claim in on him."

He was as good as his word. We hadn't finished that second coffee and he returned.

"There are no claims on him yet, but we'll have to wait until race time this afternoon. He won't be the favourite in the race, but he'll be a close second. He's up against a colt that did well in a handicap last week. His name is Good Grief. His sire was a late bloomer, so he probably will be. His sire was very good at three years old and beyond."

We piled into Bert's Land Rover and drove over to the backstretch at the track to talk to some owners of lesser horses. We talked to four owners and bought three horses: one for me, one for George and one for Robert.

"That didn't cost much," observed George. "I just spent the money I made on the claim on my old horse. I'm pleased; I'm ready to yell at a horse again. This guy is ready to race."

"Bert will arrange with John to get the horses to Peterborough," I said. "I guess we're finished here. Let's go to Peterborough to see if we can stir up some trouble there."

John was overjoyed at the new additions. "I've got Max and the young Jones boy building new stalls for all the new horses. Robert, your gelding, Amos Nandi, that arrived two weeks ago. He's racing tomorrow. I think he needs the race, but it probably won't be the best he can do. He needs a sharpener just now," he said. "Running Bear goes tomorrow, as well. I have Rebecca May in the following day. Kingston Kenny will try again, but that bout of diarrhea just about did him in completely. He's not the horse he used to be. Things are picking up. Three more horses, all of them ready to run, are arriving tomorrow."

"You'll probably need to give them the magic touch before you race them," said Robert. "Their previous trainers haven't been paying much attention to them."

"I look forward to the challenge," John said. "Come back in two weeks and I'll have them ready to go."

Amos Nandi was listed in the second race, a conditioned race. The conditions were that the horses had to be non-winners of two races this calendar year. Amos Nandi started the race strong; he gained first place easily at the start and when challenged in the back stretch he hung on against a determined challenge from the outside. Halfway down the home stretch he weakened and fell back slowly until he crossed the finish in fifth place.

"Just as I thought," said John. "Will did all he could to get him home when he did. He needed that race to tighten things up. I know he's got more left. I'll have him in the same class in two weeks. He'll be better."

Running Bear's race was the fifth, in the same class as his previous race two weeks ago. He started off well and was in third place at the rail on the first turn. Will took him wide to give him running room as they came up to the clubhouse turn. Running Bear came around the outside to gain the lead in the early stretch. He was running well but got caught by two other horses right at the wire. He ended up coming in third by a half-length. Not bad for an old horse.

Robert went to the airport and got his Spitfire ready for the fly-by in Ottawa. When he had checked that the systems were all working properly, he got in and flew to Ottawa. We stayed to watch the racing tomorrow.

Next day, the first race had George's old horse that had been claimed from him two weeks ago running. He had been dropped down to the lowest-class race on the track. George was outraged.

"Look at that," said George. "They've raced him twice in the past two weeks, and here he is for the third time. That's too much for a horse his age."

"That is a lot," I said. "I guess they're trying to make a quick buck off him."

Joe Cool, for his part, started off fourth on the rail and faded right out of any contention by the three-quarter mark. The driver pulled him up there and walked him back. Poor Joe Cool; he was blowing hard as he went past us to the barn.

The two-year-old-filly race was the top race scheduled for the day. Rebecca May made the other fillies in the race look quite outclassed. She took the lead at the start and again without urging continued to put more and more distance between herself and the others in the race. She won easily, going away by about ten lengths.

"Well," said John afterward, "I knew she was good, but that's the best of the local two-year-old fillies. She'll have to go to Bert so she can be tried against the best around."

"You must be proud of her," said George.

"Very proud," said John. "I wish I could be in Toronto to watch her, but there is just too much to do here on the farm. I'll make sure to go and see her when she gets to the top of what she can do."

Kingston Kenny was in the last race, quite reduced from the class he used to run in. Will took him to the front of the pack on the first turn and kept him there as far as he could. There was a challenge to his position on the last turn, and although he kept going to the last, he wound up third, not disgraced by any means. Two years ago, he would have destroyed this field. He had, however, proven he wasn't done yet.

George and I went to my cottage after the races; we felt we could get in some fishing tonight and early tomorrow. Robert called to say he was going to fly the Spitfire to Smith's Falls and that we should drive back by ourselves.

"How can we fish?" asked George. "The boat is in Two Moons."

"I guess you've forgotten the old cedar-strip launch," I said. "We can use that. I know it's old, but we used to use it all the time. I store it at the marina in the winter and they tune it up for spring and then take it to the cottage for me. It'll be there."

The old launch was indeed there so we loaded up and headed for Nogie's Creek. That was our favourite spot. Bass season had just started. We dropped anchor and began to cast. George caught a large crappie, then I caught another. We kept them for supper; they were good eating. Just when we were getting tired of casting, I caught a two-and-a-half-pounder. Then George caught one almost the same size. We gave up for the night and headed back to the cottage. The crappies accompanied by some mashed potatoes and carrots made a fine evening meal.

When we woke up the next morning, it was raining a steady drizzle. We decided to forgo the fishing and start for Smith's Falls right away.

"That rain is so depressing," said George, "and it looks as if it's going to last all day. That's going to slow our trip down."

As we drove along, I said to George, "Have you seen a change in Robert lately?"

"Not really," said George, "but he seemed extraordinarily preoccupied when we were stranded after the fuel ran out. I don't know what that was all about."

"Yes, that's the sort of thing I mean. We ought to ask him how he feels when we get back. Do you think that's a good idea?"

"Definitely. I like and respect Robert. We can approach it slow and easy; I wouldn't want to upset him."

"I don't like what is happening with Joe Cool," said George. "He's like an old friend. The new barn is not treating him right—he should have a dignified retirement."

"Well, that's horse racing," I said. "You should never fall in love with a horse. He's twelve years old now, and January first, he automatically becomes thirteen. He won't be able to race anymore. They're just trying to recoup their investment before it's too late."

"I know all that," said George, "but I still don't like it. They'll probably just send him to the glue factory."

"Very likely," I said. "He is, after all, a gelding, so he can't be bred. All he can do is eat for the rest of his days."

"I know," said George, "but he's provided me, at least, with a lot of entertainment. I feel I should do something."

"Well, if you feel that strongly about it," I said, "you could call John and ask him if he could try to buy him back for you. They were racing him in a three-thousand-dollar claimer. You could probably get him for less than that. All you need is the money."

"Well, I've got the money," he said. "Stop in the next town and I'll use a pay phone to call John. Might as well get it started now. Where is the next town?"

"We're about five miles from Marmora," I said.

John made his call and when he returned to the car, he said, "I feel a lot better now. John said he thought he could get Joe Cool for about fifteen hundred dollars, and he agreed to board him next year when he has to retire."

"That's good to hear," I said. "It's well after noon so why don't we have lunch here? Looks like a good restaurant just over there. We'll be in Smith's Falls for supper. I wonder what's for supper tonight? There's always lots of food, but I like more of a variety. I know that's picky beyond belief, but that's me."

CHAPTER 10

The first thing we heard when we pulled into the yard was that another girl was missing. No sign of her anywhere. A massive hunt was being set up for this evening. All volunteers were called to the local police station. The police had been busy all day doing door-to-door searches. Nothing, not even a rumour, had been produced so far. We were all very angry, but George was almost hysterical, very nearly incomprehensible. I had never seen him so upset. We made a very short process of supper and then we all drove into town to volunteer at the police station. Nearly all the able-bodied, both men and women, were gathered there to do a thorough search. The police formed us into groups and assigned us grids. There were enough of us that we were planted hardly ten feet apart. We all knocked off when it was too dark to see anymore. No one had anything to report. Everyone promised to be there at first light to start again. This latest missing girl seemed to be the last straw for most people. People were exhausted. Most people had only stopped briefly for lunch and dinner. Search parties had covered an area spanning two to three miles out of town and each grid had been thoroughly searched at least twice. Yet nothing of significance had been found.

By the third day most people had gone back to work. We three went back to the search.

"You know," said George at lunch, "I think he hid her well. I don't think she's just laying around, waiting to be found. I don't have any idea where else to search."

"It's uncanny," said Robert. "There's nothing to go on."

George looked thoughtful. "There's something that's been niggling away at my brain, but I can't quite lay my finger on it."

"I guess we might as well get back to work," I said. "We'll get back at the search when they have more to go on."

At supper, I said to Robert, "You seem to be distracted lately. What's bothering you?"

"Oh, I don't think it's anything much," he said. "I just feel sort of restless these days. I think some of it is due to Two Moons. Maybe it's the lower gravity there. Have you felt anything? I feel sort of empty and a bit lost. I can't seem to concentrate properly."

"I know what you mean," I said. "How about you, George?"

"Honestly, I can't think about anything else just now with that young girl missing. It's bothering me a lot."

"I think I've finally come to terms with the loss of my family in the war," said Robert. "They're gone. They have been for a long time now. I've grieved enough, I think. It isn't that I don't love their memory anymore. It just seems as if I should try to carry on, you see. My wife would approve, I think."

"I believe you to be right," I said. "I lost my wife under different circumstances, of course, and she's still with me in spirit, but I, too, think she would want me to carry on."

"It helps that you understand," said Robert. "That's a load off my mind. I still wish I could have done more to save them, but when I think about it rationally, I know I couldn't have.

"I was part of 11 Group, 92 Squadron; we scrambled early. The date is forever seared on my mind: September 15, 1940. It was a Sunday, maybe Jerry thought they would catch us at church. I didn't get to go to church that day—I just got to kill people. I, finally, after all this time, believe God has forgiven me. I don't know for sure, but I think my family died in the afternoon raid. Jerry got through to London in the afternoon. The sky was totally clouded over, so they just dropped their bombs anywhere. We had every plane up. There were too many."

"The Nazis were sending over wave after wave of bombers," I said. "You weren't just sitting idly by. The bomb that hit their house and killed them; they probably never even heard."

"Intellectually, I know that. I flew four sorties that day. I shot down six planes, yet somehow it has never seemed enough."

"You were awarded ever medal your government had available except the Victoria Cross, and you didn't qualify for that one. You were even shot down twice and still you continued, even though you were wounded. You were a certified ace with more than twenty kills to your credit. No one could ask more of you."

"I could. My wounds were minor. We had to do our best."

"You did," I said.

"I do feel that a tremendous load has been lifted from my shoulders in the last week or so. This new world, Two Moons, I feel, offers a great new start for mankind. I intend to build a house there and live there if it's possible."

"I think that's a good plan. I might do that myself," I said. "There is quite a community starting up there. Nice people, too."

Before lunch was over, a load of lumber came in for Dave, and with it the news that a fisherman at Lower Reach Park in Smith's

Falls had reeled in a dismembered leg. The authorities believed it to belong to the latest missing girl, June Devlin. It was very upsetting news. George went off alone; lunch was cancelled. No one could eat.

Robert, Bruce, and I got in Bruce's car and went to the park. The police had it all cordoned off and were doing their best to keep the curiosity-seekers back out of the way. They refused any help, but we could see several boats with divers and tools dragging the pond. We stayed a while and while we were there, the boats brought up two or three things that they kept well shrouded.

Driving back to the farm, Bruce said, "I've heard from my army surplus guy. He says he has found a couple of Dakota aircraft that you might be interested in. What are Dakotas?"

"You've heard us talking about DC3s—well, that's what they are. They were used extensively during the war as cargo planes. Where are they located?" I asked.

"They're at Trenton air base. You have to talk to the quartermaster, if you want to see them."

"That's about 150 miles away," I said. "I can take the plane down and take a look at them. They will have a lot of airtime on the frames and engines, but maybe one might be okay to buy."

George had disappeared so Robert and I boarded our plane at Smith's Falls airport and flew to Trenton. We found the quartermaster and were shown the planes. There were two. We looked them over well. They were both in good condition, considering the number of flying hours they had logged. We took a long time going over their logbooks.

As we were looking through the books, a fellow sauntered up to us.

"This guy might be able to tell you more," said the quartermaster. "He looked after at least one of them for a long time."

"Hello there," he said, "can I help in any way?"

"I guess you know these planes fairly well," I said, turning to him.

"Holy Mother!" he said. "You're Flying Officer Withers. I haven't seen you since we were on the air base together in England at the start of the war. I thought you were killed."

I looked at him closely. "You must be Mike Graham! I never thought we would run into each other again. You were from Winnipeg, were you not?"

"That's right, sir," he said, "but I took my last tour here and when I got out, I just stayed. There's nobody left for me in Winnipeg."

"Please don't call me 'sir' anymore," I said. "My name is Ron. I haven't been in the service for years."

"Sorry, Ron," he said. "Old habits die hard. What can I tell you about these planes? I was a mechanic on them out on the eastern front, as well. The planes both flew the Burma Hump with supplies. One of them was hit a couple of times by the Japs. Just ground fire, though, so no real damage. Are you thinking of starting a small airline? If so, do you need a mechanic?"

"First, let me introduce my friend Robert. He was in the RAF, flying Spitfires," I said, "but the answer to your question is no, about us setting up a small airline. We have a special purpose for a plane, but there may be a need for a mechanic."

"This old girl," said Mike, "is probably your best bet. She's had fewer flying hours overall and had her engines replaced last year. I know the quartermaster here wants to get rid of these planes as he feels they're taking up too much room and are worthless. Is there any possibility you could let me negotiate for you?"

"I don't see any reason not to let you do the bidding," I said. "Just let me be there to say okay to the final price."

We went into the quartermaster's office. It was clear right away that he wanted to get rid of the planes. He felt that they were a blight on his inventory. In the end, we wound up with both planes and two rebuilt engines, as well, at a completely ridiculous price. Mike proved to be a good negotiator.

We flew home. George had appeared from wherever he had been, so we told him of our day's negotiations and set up for all three of us to drive down to Trenton in the morning. Robert and I would load the spare engines and parts on the DC3s and fly the planes back to Smith's Falls. George had never flown anything like a DC3 so he would just bring the car home.

The next day at Trenton, Mike climbed in with me and acted as flight engineer on the trip back.

"We're not staying here," I told Mike when we landed. "We'll take the planes to our place in a few days when we can arrange with the OPP to give us passage along the roads. We'll tow them to a farm, but in the meanwhile, I'll show you something that is truly amazing."

We talked with Bruce, then I drove straight through to Two Moons. Mike was flabbergasted. "For now, this is secret. It will be announced to the world in September. We needed an extra plane because we got into a problem. We only have that 180 here and we had an incident where we ran out of gas far from base. We need something to respond to that sort of thing."

When Mike recovered his breath, he said, "I see the situation. I'd love to be part of this."

"Bruce Monfils is in charge," I said, "but I'm sure he will welcome an extra pair of hands. I'll introduce you at supper. We eat well here. The engines here have been altered to run on ethanol; let's hope the Dakotas won't prove to be a problem that way. We produce our own corn here—more is being planted in the ground as we speak—then we distill it. Do you think those DC3 engines can be adapted to use ethanol?"

"I think that's easily done," said Mike.

At supper, after introducing Mike to everyone, Dave came over to say that more lumber had been delivered today but that his house was still missing a roof.

"We haven't forgotten the dinner invitation, though. You're invited, as well, Mike," Dave said. "I'd like to talk to you about your war experiences. I love hearing about those days. How about tomorrow?" Dave turned back to me. "It's okay with Robert and George. I've already talked to them."

"Sounds perfect," I said. "We have a big problem right now locally, Mike. Young girls from the area are getting raped and killed. Later tonight some of us are going to do a patrol around town to see if we can spot anything going on. Would you like to join us?"

"I'd be glad to help," said Mike.

"Whoever is doing it seems to be getting bolder all the time. George used to be a detective with the Toronto police force before the war. There seems to be very little to go on at the moment, though."

After sundown, we rode into town to start a patrol. There were four of us now. We stopped in the local coffee shop to let the last of the light fade. We each took a quarter of the town and set off, slowly walking around. By three in the morning, we had seen nothing, so we went home for some well-deserved rest.

We arranged with the OPP to give us an escort to get the DC3s to the farm the next day. Mike went off with Dave to work on the big barn that we were building to serve as a hangar. Robert and George took off to do more mapping while I went with our flatbed army truck to the Smith's Falls airport, where we unloaded first one then the other spare engine we had purchased. I didn't eat lunch. I wanted to be hungry so I could appreciate Leslie's meal at supper.

When suppertime came, there was no let-down. Leslie had cooked a huge lasagna for us.

Dave and Leslie had their appliances and a generator under a big tarp. Their sleeping bags were under there, as well. They were anxious to get the house built.

"I thought you might like something different from the never-ending meat and potatoes at the farm for a change," she said. "The meals there get a little monotonous, in my opinion."

"You are definitely correct on that point," I said. "Maybe I'm just a rebel, but I like a bit more variety."

"Your rolls are nice and flaky," said George. "The best that I've had lately. I like crisp, fresh rolls."

"There's apple pie and ice cream for dessert," she said. "We imported the ice cream from outside. We wanted to try out our refrigerator. Both the refrigerator and the stove work well off the generator. We just have to remember to keep the refrigerator door closed when the generator is not running. So far we've been successful in that."

Robert took me aside after the meal. We were taking a walk along the river to settle our stomachs.

"What would you say if I said that I was thinking of asking Sue out on a date?" he asked.

"Do you mean Sue McGregor?" I replied.

"Yes. I know I'm older than she is. I'm forty-two and she's in her mid-thirties. We've both been married before," he said. "I just feel I'd like to have a companion at times."

"Sounds like a super idea," I said. "Have you said anything to her about this?"

"No, but we've talked a few times," he said. "I'm just shy, I guess. I'm way out of practice, as well. What if she says no?"

"Well, of course she could refuse," I said, "but you know the old saying, 'Nothing ventured, nothing gained!' Go ahead and ask her, you may be pleasantly surprised."

As dusk gathered, Mike joined us again to go to town and patrol. We kept to our previous patrol areas. We were used to them and did a more thorough sweep because of the familiarity. We went home at 3:00 a.m., again with nothing to show for our work.

Mid-morning, we trailered the DC3s to the farm. The OPP gave us an escort. It didn't take long, but we had a man walking at each wing tip to see that the telephone and hydro poles were far enough back. That slowed us down to a walk, but the distance was not far. Frank and Mike got to work on the engines at once to get them converted to ethanol. George and Robert went out on a mapping run, and I manned the base radio.

I met Robert after lunch, when we were heading back for the afternoon's work. "You look very pleased with yourself," I said. "What's the big smile for?"

"Well, I asked Sue out to a movie, and she said she'd love to go with me," he said.

"I thought that might be the reason for the smile. I bet she's not worried about the age difference, either."

"You were right— the age difference wasn't part of the conversation. On another subject, I think we've done enough mapping from the skies for now. We need crews in the jeeps to drive places to get exact measures."

"Let's talk to Bruce at supper and see what he thinks," I said.

"Why don't you guys decide among yourselves what to do about the mapping?" Bruce said that evening when we brought it up over dinner. "You've done a great job so far. I have some big brains from a couple of the universities coming here next week, so I'll be pretty busy with them."

"Okay," I said, "leave it with us. We'll work it out and let you know. Are these 'big brains' coming for any particular reason?"

"I'm just trying to pave the way to announce Two Moons to the world. I need to get academia on our side," he said.

When George and Robert and I were together, I asked, "What can we do to get more detail into the maps? Bruce said for us to decide and to go ahead."

"My proposal, as you already know," said Robert, "is that we get some jeeps and head out on land. Keep in touch by radio and explore by jeep and by foot."

"What do you think, George?" I asked.

"I like Robert's suggestion. We can start Monday, if you like, but I think we should see if there are more surplus jeeps available for purchase."

"The jeeps are getting a lot of use," I said. "I agree we should buy three or four more, if they are available."

CHAPTER 11

We decided to split up into two groups of two people to a jeep and each work a different area to get a closer look at the land from that perspective. We would run the single-sideband radios off the generator on the jeep. That way we could be in touch with each other all the time. Mike and I would be in one jeep, with George and Robert in the other.

"I wonder if I might make a suggestion," said Mike. "I like hot food best. They showed us a way to make a simple stove when I was overseas. This was meant as a basic survival thing but it sort of applies. It's called a rocket stove. You just need twenty-five to thirty bricks and some twigs. I think this bamboo stuff would work well. You can't use large pieces of wood; small twigs work the best."

"Is it hard to build?" asked George.

"No, quite simple," said Mike. "You can build it in about five minutes and take it down in as short a time. It gives off a hot fire. Because the ventilation sort of roars up the flue at a fast rate, it is sometimes called a rocket stove. It makes a noise like a rocket. I see a small pile of bricks alongside that Quonset hut there. Are we allowed to use some?"

"Yes, we can use them," I said. "I know what they were originally for and they're no longer needed."

“Let me quickly show you,” he said. “It will take about five minutes as I mentioned, then we can have hot food for lunch.”

As he said, it took him about five minutes to successfully make a hot fire. We gathered some bricks and food from the kitchen and loaded them into the jeeps.

“Very simple and easy,” said George, “but why not use bigger pieces of wood?”

“Bigger pieces tend to choke the fire out,” said Mike. “The firebox is too small for bigger wood. Dry pine needles are a good fire starter. This little stove uses very few resources, which is the other thing working in its favour.”

“I’m all for it,” said George. “To change the subject, though, I talked to the police chief last night. He said they had recovered more body parts from the pond. The murderer appears to have used an axe to cut her up. No fingerprints were found, so he used gloves. The police think she was chloroformed, then dragged to an old, abandoned house outside of town along the railroad tracks. We’ll have to keep up our vigilance.”

Mike and I went north and George and Robert south. We were able to mark the shallow points of rivers as places we could cross easily. We discovered more areas where the bamboo-type grasses were growing and marked the rivers’ courses in more detail. For the most part, the land was open and flat. There were small rises and falls in the terrain itself, but it was quite level otherwise.

At supper Dave and Leslie again came to eat with us in the main farm building.

“We’ve got some of the crops in already,” said Dave. “I’ve had a lot of help. We have about a hundred acres of corn and about fifty acres of grain crops in. Leslie suggested that we use the ancient grains as this land is quite pure. The engineered grains, we think, are not as healthy. Our bodies and those of the cattle have used these grains for 50,000 years and we think they are healthier. Just for Leslie, I put in about fifty acres of Semolina. She loves pasta. We have a pasta maker so we can make our own."

"Looks as if you have things well in hand," I said. "What's next on the agenda?"

"Bruce wants me to use the shovel part of the tractor to dig a sewer to a large holding tank and weeping bed. I'm going to start that tomorrow."

Our night patrol started as usual: Mike, George, Robert and I each took an area of town to patrol. Shortly after midnight, George saw a man sneaking around. The man had come out of a business through a window. He was carrying a big bundle. George followed him to a house and waited until the lights went out, then he went to the police station and reported the incident. The police knew the residence as a place they had long suspected of participating in crimes of that sort. They called the business owner to come to his business and see if anything was missing. At the same time, they surrounded the house that the thief had entered and waited for the business owner's report. There were indeed many things missing, including the cash float, which had been hidden. The police then arrested four people who lived in the house, and, upon searching the premises, they found all the missing merchandise, as well as things that had gone missing from other businesses over the past little while.

George was hailed as a hero. The night had been an adventurous one, but we were still no closer to catching the killer.

At breakfast, Bruce stood and, in a loud voice, said, "I have a grave announcement to make. The astronomers and others have arrived from the university. They tell us that a very large meteor has been observed heading straight toward Earth. The announcement will be on the radio and television on today's news. The populace is going to be told that the meteor will miss the Earth, but our friends say this is a lie. The leaders do not want the populace to panic. The meteor will be a direct hit. All that we know will be destroyed. We, however, have a way to avoid it; most people have nothing. We must get friends and loved ones here if we can, to save them. We have two telephone lines here for your use. Albert and Bonnie next door have another. Our priority above all else is to save as many as we can."

I was shaken to the roots of my soul. I volunteered to go to Albert and Bonnie's and ask to use their telephone. They believed me immediately and set about calling their relatives. When they were done, I started by telephoning my sons in Toronto. They had heard the news and were willing to listen me and believed what I said. I told them to leave as soon as possible and directed them on how to find us. I told them not to be more than a week getting here.

Next, I called my friend and horse trainer, John. He was skeptical but agreed that we were not always told the truth. I said that he could always take his stuff back home if I had it wrong. I asked him to bring all the horses and equipment that he could and to leave now.

Next, I called Dan, Marie and their families in Chapleau. They had farther to come and less time to get ready. Dan argued some but, in the end, saw the wisdom in starting out immediately. I asked him to bring all the dogs. They would be great guards.

My friends in Prince Edward Island were next. I asked Randy to bring all his horses, as well, and set out as soon as he could. He had a lot of things to bring from the farm. I told him to rent a transport trailer or two, and if he couldn't afford it, then he should tell me, and I would arrange for the money to be available. I pointed out that money would soon be worth nothing.

What amazed me most was that everyone had taken my word for what was happening. The authorities were telling everyone not to panic—the meteor would miss. I guess they were worried that everything would turn to chaos, and since we were all doomed anyway, calm was needed for now.

Robert and George were waiting when I returned.

"I contacted the only people I have that I still consider friends," George said, "and Robert here has nobody in this country, so we're done. Dave, too, has been in touch with his extensive family in and around Peterborough. Some have concerns. I think we could help by being in Peterborough. What do you say we fly there now and give them as much help as we can?"

"That sounds like a good idea," I said, "then we can fly on to Chapleau and help there. Then on to Toronto. I must remember before we leave to talk to Bert and warn him, as well."

I went back inside and found a telephone, but it was currently being used. It took about ten minutes until I was able to make my call to my Toronto trainer, Bert. He was not convinced, but I told him to remember he could always go back if it didn't happen. Better to be safe than sorry.

With Robert doing the flying, we headed for Peterborough. Morag, my housekeeper, refused to budge. We told her she would die if she didn't heed our warning, but she was adamant that she was staying. Dave's brother's family understood and believed us. We helped them to pack and then we moved on to several other families that we knew well. The guy who ran the flying school wanted to see our set-up as he called it, so he took a Cessna 150 and flew to Smith's Falls.

Our next stop was Chapleau. Marie, Dan and Betty, the adults, questioned us closely, but agreed to leave. The dogs all fit in the bed of their pickup. With five dogs it was a tight fit, but they would have to endure it for a couple of days.

In Toronto, my sons had already packed up; they would start for Smith's Falls tomorrow. Bert still did not want to believe us about Two Moons or that the meteor was actually going to hit Earth. All three of us took turns trying to convince him. I finally said, "Would you be more likely to believe us if you came to Smith's Falls and saw for yourself what we have discovered and talked to some of the astronomers?"

"Okay," he said, "fine. Can we go today? I have a big race tomorrow."

We agreed and we all went to the airport and flew to Smith's Falls. On seeing Two Moons, Bert was convinced. He agreed to come at once. We flew him back to Toronto so he could pack up.

Next morning, we flew to Prince Edward Island. Randy met us at the airport. He was upset. He wanted to believe us, but there were so many people in his extended family and many did not believe. They didn't want to uproot. We went to his farm and talked to some of his close family members. We finally had to use the same strategy with him as with Bert. We flew Randy and his wife to Smith's Falls. They talked to all the scientists, as well as Dave and Leslie and Albert and Bonnie. They were finally convinced. We flew them back to Prince Edward Island; time was ticking. They had to get their packing underway as soon as possible. We stayed overnight to help as much as we could.

We arrived in Smith's Falls to find that my sons had arrived that morning. I introduced them to Bruce and his friends.

"Bruce," I said, "Malcolm, here, is a chartered accountant. He would be a good person to add to your inventory team. My son James is a lawyer."

"Malcolm, what a pleasant addition to the team. Sue is trying her best at keeping up with our inventory, but I have a feeling that is about to become overwhelming. Could you find her and come here, and we'll discuss things?

"James," he said, "I will be needing a lot of legal advice. I had a kind of charter drawn up a few years ago, but it's awkward. I don't foresee much of a problem because we'll soon be cut off from the rest of the world, but one never knows for sure. Your father can show you around and see that you get settled. I need to get all my equipment over to Two Moons as soon as I can, or we'll lose everything."

I found my sons and their families a spot to camp near one of the Quonset huts. They were well prepared. They had bought with them a couple of large tents, as well as sleeping bags.

James said, "I wondered how we could escape a meteor strike. Now I see what you were talking about. It's hard to believe, but I'm so grateful we listened to you."

Mid-afternoon, John arrived. He had come with a huge horse box filled with the cream of his stable. Will, Max and the rest of the crew had arrived in a big cube van, stuffed to the gills with everything they could think to bring with them. Dave happened to be there as they drove through to Two Moons.

I introduced everyone. Dave, of course, knew John well. He said, "I've got a pasture where you can put the mares and fillies, but nowhere for the stallions at the moment."

I pulled Will aside and said, "I'll lead you to our wire supply and you and Max can start making some small enclosures for the stallions. Dave will show you were to build the fences."

The whole fleet of trucks followed Dave in a jeep down and across the ford to his place. It looked like a major parade. John was blown away. He decided to go back to Peterborough the next day to gather as many belongings as possible. It took the rest of the afternoon to get the horses settled. The whole crew worked long into the evening hours setting up fence.

John's men curled up where they were and fell asleep. Early the next morning, they finished the fencing. John had left early with the young Jones kid as his only crew.

Unexpectedly, our friend, the flying school owner from Peterborough, arrived with his 150, as well as a second one flown by his assistant. They asked the OPP to let them trailer the planes from the Smith's Falls airport to the farm. We left them to it and made phone calls to our various other friends and family members to see how they were getting on. We couldn't get in touch with our group from Chapleau, so we had to assume they were on their way. There was no answer in PEI, either. We took that to be good news, as well. It would have been nice to be able to contact them on the road, but there was no way to do that.

Just before supper we had a call from the Chapleau group. They had reached Lindsay and asked if someone would stay up to greet them when they arrived.

George and I stayed up. Robert was tired from all the flying. When they arrived, I showed them to a spot near where my boys and their families were staying, but not close enough to wake them. They had a couple of tents, as well. The kids were very excited and at first could not get to sleep.

"This is just like a science fiction story," commented Jimmy, "with two moons up there."

"I guess it is, in a way," I said, "but this is real."

All the kids finally ran out of energy and pretty much collapsed where they were. The dogs took longer, but finally accepted their new circumstances and they, too, lay down to sleep. George and I went back to our beds for a few hours' rest.

Bruce had started the process of getting his machinery and lab moved to Two Moons; he still needed a couple of days to finish. He had to be prepared to close the gate solidly when the time came.

We were late getting to breakfast. My sons and their families had made friends with Marie, Dan and the kids. My grandchildren were practically the same ages as the kids from the Chapleau group and they obviously got on very well together.

Jimmy came over to where I was sitting and said, "I like your grandkids. They're nice and not a bit snobbish. I thought since they came from Toronto they might be."

"Thank you," I said. "I guess we all come from Two Moons now."

"Dan and I are going to help Mr. Monfils this morning, then Dave wants us to go look at a spot over near him," said Jimmy. "He thinks we could settle there."

"Sounds good to me," I said. "See you at supper!"

Since it was going to be a busy day, I lingered over my coffee. While I sat, I closed my eyes, and said a small prayer of thanks to God that all my family and friends were safe.

CHAPTER 12

The Smith's Falls chief of police strode into the house as I was finishing my morning coffee. He was very agitated. He told us another teenage girl had a narrow escape the night before. She had been out with her girlfriends and had been within a couple of blocks of home when she was grabbed. A cloth with chloroform had been put over her mouth but she had stomped hard on the assailant's instep and had managed to escape and reach home. Her dad had taken off after the man and had come close to catching him. He had seen the man from a distance but was unable to identify the person.

He said to me, "The OPP have okayed early tomorrow morning to trailer the aircraft from the Smith's Falls airport to here. I have detailed one of my men to help."

"Thanks for coming out," I said to the chief. "We appreciate you keeping us up to date."

"It's the least I can do," he said, "after all the help you've given us."

I went to see how my sons' families were getting along. Marie was sitting with both my daughters-in-law, with the younger children playing nearby.

"I see you've met," I said. "How are you handling the shock of being uprooted?"

"It's quite a shock," said June. "Marie here tells us she came all the way from Chapleau. I never even heard of the place before, but she's told us where it is and how you met."

"This place is fascinating," said Sandra. "I do hope we will be able to return to our homes, but I like it here."

"Unfortunately," I said, "we will probably be here for the rest of our lives, but we should be safe here. It looks as if good old Earth is going to have a severe shock and may even be turned into a minor sun. How are things with you, Marie?"

"Topsy-turvy," she said. "I talked to a lot of people this morning, including some of your experts. I think we made the right move. Your friend Dave is going to show us a spot this afternoon where he says we can settle. Dan and Jimmy are helping move some things this morning."

"Jimmy's a bit young for that, isn't he" I said. "He doesn't have to work that hard."

"Let him do his turn," she said. "He's quite strong and was eager to help."

"Okay, but don't let him overdo things," I said. "We're getting a lot more help all the time. Some of the townspeople arrived today. About a hundred, I'd guess. Most of them probably aren't used to roughing it. Maybe you can help where you can."

I went to work with the crew getting Bruce's entire operation moved over to Two Moons. More people arrived: some from town, and some university people who knew about us. The townspeople seemed to fall into two groups. The first group was composed of people who appreciated what they saw. These people, quite often, went away, then came back later with tools, cooking utensils, and bedding or sleeping bags. The other group refused to believe what they saw, it seemed. They just went away, shaking their heads, and never returned.

Lunch proved to be a time when everything looked like it was going to crash and burn. It was our first meal cooked entirely on Two Moons. Bruce had gotten hold of ten stoves and had recruited ten women to do the main cooking. Each woman had found someone else to help at the stove and a couple of older kids or young adults had been press-ganged into cutting up veggies and making sandwiches.

Eventually everybody got a bowl of soup and a sandwich or two. Some of the newcomers tried to get away with a bit of hoarding, which was generally frowned upon, but they persisted anyhow. Some took three or four sandwiches. Nobody seemed to realize that there were no refrigerators to store anything and the extra they had taken would only rot.

I met Dave as he was heading to work on the sewage system.

"How is the digging going?" I asked. "I haven't had time to keep up with the latrine work."

"I have a crew following me," he said. "They're making framing as fast as I dig. Tomorrow they're going to start pouring concrete to fix the shape of the sewers. Some men are working in that second Quonset hut to make huge bathrooms—one for women, one for men. There will be about fifty toilets on each side with a communal shower room at each end. We have running water already. Cold from the falls, but it has good pressure. The toilet stalls will be in two rows on both the women and men's sides. They'll be pretty crude for a while, just a platform with a seat on top. We'll have the open sewer covered by next week."

"Are there any plans in place for making hot water?" I said. "I hate cold showers."

"We acquired a couple of plumbers from the people who have come from town. They not only brought much needed knowledge, but some equipment as well. We should have hot water as soon as next week. Everybody is working hard."

Leslie was in the main compound as well. I said hello.

"Can we get more lumber?" she asked. "I've made an incubation box for our chickens and the other farmers with chickens want to build one, as well."

"I'll speak to Bruce," I said, "but if he's too busy I'll see to it myself. I agree we need as much lumber as we can get. Time is short and the people on Earth are still unbelieving. Why the incubator box?"

"We're going to need a lot more chickens, not to mention eggs for breakfasts and baking. I've got forty eggs in the box we built already, ready to incubate and hatch I hope, but we need lots more."

Things were happening faster than I had anticipated. I went to see Bruce, who was being run off his feet. Everything got dumped on him.

"I'm glad you came by," he said. "I need you to coordinate all the things that we need. Buy whatever is necessary. Pay for it if you can or ask me for money. Do whatever is needed. I need to get my equipment up and working here within two weeks or all will be lost. I asked George to look after security and a couple of other things. Albert is going to coordinate the farms. I asked Robert to look after our planes and transportation in general. I've also asked Bonnie to look after feeding the flock. Are you okay with being my right-hand man so I can work in peace?"

"Absolutely. I'll do my best," I said. I called the lumber yard and asked them how much they wanted for their entire stock of lumber and when they could deliver. The dollar amount when they called me back was a bit staggering, but I wrote a cheque, went to the bank, certified it, and took it to them. The cheque emptied my bank account. I had sold all my stocks, but it was too late to sell any of my properties. They promised to start delivery tomorrow. I then went to all the appliance stores in town and bought up as much equipment as possible, putting it on Bruce's tab. Next stop was the farm equipment manufacturer.

Mid-afternoon, Albert and Bonnie brought by two of their farmer friends. These people were beef farmers and had other domesticated animals, as well. They took to the place, and Albert went back to their farm with them to salvage what they could and bring it over. These latest people were the second farmers that Albert and Bonnie had brought in today. This time, Albert and his friend drove his friends' whole herd in and then drove it south toward the portage.

I asked him what he was going to do to keep the cattle together.

"Your friends from Peterborough have built a very large enclosed pasture for the cows," he said. "We're going to paint the sides of the cows with stripes in different colours to show who owns what. Pigs are going to be handled differently. We're building sturdier pens for them. No one wants a bunch of feral pigs around. They're dangerous."

Bonnie drove their pickup in to the compound. It had a large box on the back, with a load of squawking chickens inside. They headed south toward the portage, as well.

Albert continued, "We've set up a headquarters for the farm folk near your friend Dave's place. That's so we can be near Leslie, our only large animal vet so far. If you need us that's where you'll likely find us."

Some farm equipment started to arrive that afternoon, so I directed them to Dave's. Wonder of wonders, the first load of lumber arrived, as well. Late in the day, Bert Mason, our Toronto trainer, arrived with one large transport truck filled with horses and another with equipment. He brought many sulkies, as well as harnesses. I sent him to Dave's place. John would oversee the horses and such when he got back with his second load. He could probably use the paint scheme to identify the different owners of the horses, too. Things were happening fast. More people from town arrived and were looked after.

Suppertime arrived. The food was roast of pork with potatoes and veggies. There was a small roast of beef for those who didn't like pork. The same people who had displayed hoarding tendencies at lunch were back at it at supper. The cooks had been warned about the greed and as a result a list was made. After supper, George and I took them aside, one group at a time, and talked about hoarding and taking more than one's fill. There was not much reaction. Most of the people involved felt they were entitled to all they could get away with.

I said to George afterward, "What can we do about this kind of behaviour?"

"I think we should talk to Bruce about it, but my gut reaction is, who needs these people? We certainly don't."

"You mean we should just kick them back outside and let them die?"

"That would be my solution. I've seen this type of behaviour time after time. It's petty crime. They don't care. I bet most are welfare cheaters, as well. They'll always be the same. We don't need them here."

"That seems kind of drastic," I said. "There must be something else that can be done."

"In my experience, they'll never change. It could be the death of us all, if carried to the extreme. And believe me, they will carry it that far."

The next morning, more lumber and farm machinery arrived, and so did our friends from PEI. I was very pleased to see Randy and his family. He had brought with him several other people I didn't know. I made them all feel welcome and sent them on to Albert to get them set up with a temporary place to stay. I explained what was going on and what we could use some help with. They all promised to help out wherever they could.

Marie and clan had moved to Dave's area, as well. She found me staring after the Prince Edward Island group.

"We've decided what we would like to do here," said Marie. "We've always been into berries and fruit, as well as preserves, so we'd like to build up that industry as much as we can. We should be able to make a living off it. Do you know who we should talk to about that?"

"I guess you should talk to me first, which you are doing," I said, "but the next person you talk to should be Peter; he's our plant specialist. Let's go find him and I'll introduce him to you."

Peter was overjoyed that someone wanted to focus on berries. He suggested other fruit they could grow, as well. Marie was agreeable to all his suggestions.

Dave's brother, Raymond, and his family arrived, accompanied by John on his second trip back. They had joined up in Peterborough. They were delayed on account of driving around and picking up Gransden relatives. John's large horse trailer was full of horses. He also had a full transport trailer with everything one could think of in it. In total, there were five cars full of people and goods, plus John. I sent them on to Dave's farm.

I asked around for Arnie, one of our two army veterans from Petawawa. We needed more Quonset huts set up. I got together three of the new people to help him. When I found him, finally, I told him what was needed. He said he would start on one today. I asked him to keep building until all the huts were erected.

George came up to me as another load of lumber arrived. "You'll never guess," he said. "We've had a bit of luck in the greed department. The worst person by far was that young woman who totally ignored us. She was the common-law wife of the head plumber we have. One of the townsfolk. I guess she whined too much to him last night, so he drove her back to town and told her to stay there. He doesn't want anything more to do with her."

Albert drove up from the area of Dave's farm where he had set up a sort of office to oversee the farming operations. "That young feller from Prince Edward Island and his bunch are certainly go-getters. They were after me first thing this morning. They wanted to know where they could have some land. I showed him a huge patch quite a piece away from other projects. He wants to start planting potatoes this afternoon. I told him to go ahead and got him a tractor and some machinery to get him started."

Marie and Peter returned from their expedition around Two Moons to find a place they liked. Marie felt she had found the ideal spot but wanted to talk to Dan, her brother-in-law, first, to get his opinion. It was on the east side of the river and south of the portage from Dave's area. The land got narrower on that side, but there was plenty of room for what they needed. The river widened south of that into a big lake. The lake looked deep. The small mountains on the east closed in down there and Marie felt almost at home.

Lunch was better organized today. Lots more soup and heaps of sandwiches of all sorts: tomato, cucumber, and different types of meat. No egg. I was told that all unnecessary eggs were being set to be incubated. No excessive hoarding or greed was seen. Mike sat down with me. He looked exhausted.

"What have you been doing?" I asked. "You look worn out."

"I've been kept constantly busy demonstrating rocket stoves. We've come up with a lot of improvements. We now have a design with a small oven inside. Nearly every family group has one now. I'm going to relax a bit and then go help the Quonset hut builders."

"Maybe, instead, you could grab a man or two and use the big flatbed truck to drive out to the nearest bamboo growth. We will need lots of fuel for these stoves, and we don't have wood. Tomorrow you could do the same by going back to the Earth side and getting lots of dead wood. Don't get green wood, though. There should be lots lying around in the local forests. Ask Albert what he would suggest."

"That's a good idea. I wondered what to do about that. I'll just have another cup of coffee and then I'll get on it. I guess if that meteor hits, there will be no more coffee after that."

Late afternoon, Marie and Dan came driving back through the gate from Smith's Falls. They were towing a small fishing boat with a ten-horsepower motor on it and a canoe tied to the top.

"Lots of used boats around here. I guess a lot of residents fish the Rideau," Dan said. "I might get another tomorrow. The people we got these from didn't charge too much."

"I never thought of that," I said. "Too much on my mind, I guess. I'll talk to Bruce and see if we can get some money for a couple more."

"That's okay," said Dan. "I've got lots of money left; I'll get more, and we can square up later. Money won't be worth anything very soon anyway. I guess you heard we've found an ideal spot to settle. Almost like home. It even has a cave and everything."

What else haven't we thought of? I thought to myself. Nothing vital, I hoped. Everyone was working very hard. Things were going smoothly. I hoped we could all get along. Was that too much to ask?

Bruce was in a conference with some university people. I wondered what they were discussing.

Supper, when it was served, was mostly roast pork again, but with lots of vegetables and abundant fruit for dessert, as well as pie. Monotonous food but we had a good supply of it.

CHAPTER 13

The university people had heard from their colleagues. The meteor was not only going to hit Earth square on, but had a shower of other meteors around it. These smaller ones could be deadly by themselves. Some of the smaller ones were ahead of the largest and would hit as soon as next week. People from the university that had talked to our people and believed us had chartered a plane to get here. Many were in a state of panic. They told us that the first contingent would be here later today. I was asked to take the troop truck and the flatbed to pick them up. Mike had disappeared early in the flatbed with Albert to find dead wood for the rocket stoves. I hoped he would be back in time for the airport pickup.

I went over to the main area of Two Moons where most of the activity was taking place. A man was sitting at the picnic tables, looking very disheartened.

"How are things going for you?" I asked.

"Not so bad as it might seem," he said. "I just feel there's nothing here for my talents. I've been helping out at several spots, mostly building, but that's kind of boring. Don't get me wrong, I'm thankful to be here with my family. I just feel useless."

"You're from town, I guess?" I said. "What did you do before you came here?"

"My name is Max Owens. I owned a real estate firm. That's not of any use here. It might be twenty years from now, but not in the near future."

"You're right in that everything is free here at the moment," I said. "But I think you may have solved a problem that I hadn't realized we had. Maybe even two problems."

"What do you mean?" he asked.

"Do you have one of those long tape measures and a calculator?"

"Yes, my calculator is old and mechanical, not electric, but I do have a tape."

"Good," I exclaimed. "Here's what I suggest. Do you see this area, stretching from here, south along the beach and lake? It's about two miles wide here and gets a little narrower, but not much, to the south."

"Yes, it's got a lot of junk spread around in it just now, but I see the area you mean."

"Sooner or later we will need housing, later even shops and maybe someday a small manufacturing plant. I'd like you to pretend you're the town planner. Lay out roads, extra wide would bc best, lay out housing lots at least two acres each. We'll need lots with one-bedroom houses, other houses with at least two bedrooms and a few executive-type houses. There should be a place for a strip mall with shops and maybe some individual businesses. Could you lay out something like that?"

"I'd love to," he said. "When do I start?"

"Now, if you want. If you need anything, just find me and ask."

There was a big commotion near the gate. A huge flock of sheep were coming through, driven by five border collies. I didn't see the owner at first; he was hidden in the melee.

Finally, I got near him and yelled for him to turn south. He whistled at the dogs. All their heads turned to him. He made some gestures and added more whistles. They leapt to work and in a noticeably short time had the flock going in the right direction. He had a helper with him, whom I hadn't noticed earlier. I pulled him aside and told him what to look for.

One of the men reported to me. He had been told to tell me when the latrine Quonset hut was finished on the inside. I went to inspect what they had done and was amazed. There was a big central aisle, with men directed to one side and women to the other. Each side had a large shower area at the front end with six shower heads attached to each wall and a drain for the wastewater. It was connected to the sewer that the men had dug.

The sewer was lined with concrete and sloped down through the latrine area. The latrine area had a smaller aisle down the middle with ten stalls on each side. Each stall had a platform with a toilet seat. These were positioned directly over the concrete sewer. The tops of the sewer were covered with concrete fitted slabs. No need to flush here: everything went straight into the sewer.

At the other end of the building there were ten sinks for washing hands.

"A marvel of engineering," I said. "Who do we have to thank for all this?"

"Manny Wisnewski, our plumber from town," he said. "He did a super job."

As I was crossing back to the tables to get some lunch, Albert and Mike returned. They had a truckload of cedar rails they'd procured from an old fence. They were nice and dry and could be used as fire starters.

I told Albert to expect the sheep man and his herd. He drove off south in a jeep. Then I told Mike I needed him to drive the flatbed out to the airport to pick up the university types who were arriving. He had a quick lunch and started unloading the flatbed.

Marie and Dan were just behind them coming through the gate. They had bought two canoes and a large runabout with a thirty-five-horsepower outboard. They had read the local advertisements in the town paper and had little trouble finding what they wanted. They waved and headed south to their chosen spot.

I asked around to see where I could find Manny Wisnewski. I found him in his new latrine.

"You did a super job on the facilities in this hut," I said. "Would you be interested in another job?"

"I can do my best, but if it isn't plumbing, I don't know much else," he said.

"It's similar," I said, "but no plumbing just yet. Can you set up the new hut next door? For now, it needs to serve as sleeping accommodations. The hangar needs the same treatment. Most people are just sleeping on the ground. I would like this new Quonset hut to be men on one side, and women and kids on the other. As many spaces as we can fit in just now."

"I can do that all right," he said. "I'll get my crew and start tomorrow."

As I was heading back to see Bruce and report what was happening, two more trucks loaded with lumber came in from the lumber yard in town. I figured we must have nearly all their stock by now. I had negotiated for all the nails and equipment I could get. They were bringing that, as well. Upon looking through the merchandise that had just been shipped, I saw huge boxes of nails. All appeared to be in order.

I flagged down a couple of young teenage girls who were standing around and sent them to find my bean-counter son, Malcolm. A short time later he arrived and asked me what I had on my mind.

"How are you and Sue getting along with the inventory?" I asked

"We have two other women working with us, but it's a huge task," he said.

"I have a different idea. It's much more important. You're the accountant, so you'll see what I'm talking about. Keep your records but change your focus to the following: I want you to take over as lead accountant. Don't hurt Sue's feelings, though; she's worked very hard. Just tell her I asked you to handle it.

"First, I want you to organize an inventory of all the people we have here, and a record of what they have worked at and when they arrived. You're going to be Internal Revenue, I guess. Second, I want to know the hours worked by each. We don't have a currency yet. For now, it will be hours worked. We will start with five units—or dollars, if you like— per hour. Dollars will be understood easier. Five dollars for unskilled labour, six for skilled labour and farmers, seven for supervisors, and eight for university folks.

"These we will use as credits. Those who work hardest, as shown by the number of credits they have, will get priority when it comes to housing and other things. This should help with getting people working, and later when we build houses, we can use that as part of the criteria."

"Sounds like a good plan, Pop," he said. "I'll start on it right away."

"You'll probably need more help. Just recruit whomever you need."

Reverend Stead came through the gate with a small convoy of seven cars, each one filled to the brim. The people got out of the cars and formed a small circle and knelt to pray. Some of the townspeople joined the circle. I saw George nearby, so I asked him if he would help settle Reverend Stead's people.

Albert had just come back from the Earth-side farm. He had answered the phone there. A farmer on the next concession needed help. He could get here but he had no way to bring his stock. There were two empty transport trucks sitting idle. I told Albert to get Jim and take the two trucks to collect the herd. We could sluice them out with the hose later. We could always use more farmers with livestock. Feeding the people who were still coming in, large groups of them, would have to be addressed somehow.

Mike was ready to go to the airport; he had found out that the university people had landed and were waiting to be picked up. He had the flatbed. I commandeered the troop transport and went with him to the airport. The plane was a DC3 like the ones we owned. It had about twenty passengers, half of whom were children. It also had boxes and boxes of books. University texts, by the look of it. We loaded all the books and luggage on the flatbed and got the people loaded onto the troop carrier. Before we had everything aboard, the plane had taken off again. The person who seemed to oversee the group said that the plane would be back later in the evening with another load of people. The children were a very sober-looking lot. They were obviously unsure of the future, but when we drove into Two Moons, their faces brightened and they took immediate interest in the surroundings.

Albert returned soon after with the farmer and all his cattle. He unloaded right away explaining that there was a sheep farmer with a flock who wanted to come in, as well. He quickly sluiced the trucks and left again.

Dave flopped down beside me at supper. He looked exhausted. "I can't even get started at building my house yet. I've got all the pieces now, but there are too many other things to do," he said. "All these herds and flocks we've had coming in has stretched us to the breaking point. We have most of the wire for the enclosures up. The men have been working almost round the clock. Leslie and Bonnie went into town this morning and bought a lot of different colours of paint so the animals can be tagged."

"That's good news," I said. "I think there is another sheep herd coming later today. Should I send them straight down?"

"If we can, I'd like to hold them this side of the ford for now until we get some paint on them. That would be best. We'll need another large fenced area for them. Do they have herder dogs with them?"

"I don't know. When they get here, I'll find out."

A woman remained on the Earth-side farm to man the phones while waiting for the call from the airport with the second load of professorial types and their families. She came to me with the news that they were ready for transport, so Mike and I got in the trucks and went to get them. This time the group consisted mainly of adults, with a couple of older teens. They had brought more books with them, as well, but not nearly as many this time. The loading was quicker, but even so, the plane had again taken off before we had finished. One man who identified himself as an astronomer urged us to hasten. He said they had detected a small meteor that looked like it was headed straight for us. We drove back to the farm in a quiet, thoughtful mood. The man went straight to Bruce and his council with his observation.

As we were unloading, four police cars came storming through the gate with sirens wailing. Each car had a police officer and his family in it. The chief headed toward Bruce, yelling that the gate must be closed now. Bruce was ready. He raced to his controls and activated the closing. The gate slid smoothly closed. Bruce had tested that the controls on this side of the gate worked well over the past few days.

We continued unloading and finding the newcomers places to lay their heads. Within a half hour Bruce announced that there had been a seismic event. We had felt nothing. Bruce thought it may have happened on Earth near our location. The gate was left closed. By morning, Earth time, no further seismic events had been recorded so Bruce slowly opened the gate. The police chief and one of his men had volunteered to check things out.

They cautiously ventured out and returned after a short time to report that all the townspeople who had remained on Earth were dead. People were found collapsed all over town. They had no visible wounds but were deceased.

Reverend Stead and many of the townsfolk who were on Two Moons with us started praying for the huge loss of life. The people here slowly gathered with Reverend Stead. Some were outwardly very upset, crying and screaming about lost relatives. Some had lost parents, some had lost brothers and sisters. The chaos went on for two hours until finally peace was restored. Those who were able to handle the news better were helping others cope. Some were praying together, others just clinging to each other. Some of the children were coping better than their parents. They were providing a shoulder for their parents to cry on when their parents were at a loss for what to do.

The phones and electricity were not working on Earth, so I drove to the airport to see if the third planeload of people had managed to arrive from Toronto. Albert took a man with him and went to check on the nearby farms. The astronomers and a medical doctor went to Smith's Falls to see if they could locate the point of impact and make another sweep for possible survivors. I got to the airport and, miraculously, the plane was there and all the passengers were okay. The pilot told me there was a large crater to the southwest of town. I radioed to the farm for the flatbed and passed on the news of the crater.

At the same time as we returned to Two Moons, Albert returned, as well, with another of his farmer friends, who now wanted to come to live here. I sent Albert off with a couple of transport drivers to bring back as much of his friend's herd and equipment as they could. The doctor who had gone into Smith's Falls reported that the population had died of asphyxiation. The meteor blast had sucked all the air out of the nearby area. The astronomer returned with the opinion that we had approximately twenty to thirty hours before the main meteor hit. It was about ten percent of the size of Earth's moon and would completely wipe out Earth and maybe even turn it into a minor sun. We rounded up as much as we could salvage from town. Albert returned with his friend and his animals. He also brought with him several other people who had previously refused our offer of sanctuary. They were now believers.

The idea of making a major sweep for survivors got underway. Albert and two other local farmers each took a jeep and, along with another man, set out to scour the area.

They returned in a few hours with loaded jeeps. The people they had found had abandoned most of their goods and come as they were. A few brought extra clothing and a sleeping bag and some camp equipment, but they were mostly empty-handed. They joined the crowd around Reverend Stead. It seemed as if the crowd of believers in God had grown enormously. There was much weeping and regret for what could have been.

With nothing more that we could think of to do, we shut the gate and waited for the big event. Most people kept busy at the tasks that they were working at. A new Quonset hut was being set up in the area we were going to build the town. I kicked them out of the area.

CHAPTER 14

The evening had been an intense one. With the morning, the astronomers went back through the gate to the Earth side. They wanted to get some final observations in before the meteor struck. The various work crews around Two Moons kept to their chosen or assigned tasks. There was a general quietness about the place—people maybe thinking of those left behind, or perhaps counting their blessings for having come here. Many were still too traumatized to do anything but sit.

John and Bert sought me out in the early afternoon.

"Are we going to have to retrain our horses to be beasts of burden now?" asked John.

"That wasn't my original thought," I said. "One of my main reasons for getting as many as we could over here was to keep them from dying. Some of them are like old friends and I thought they could eventually supply entertainment for us, as well. What I suggest is that when everything settles down, if it ever does, you and your flock could set up a track nearby and run some races occasionally. Do you think that would be possible?"

"We have about thirty-five racing horses here, so it could happen. A few are pretty useless for racing, but the mares could be bred for a future generation of horses. Three or four races on an afternoon's card could be done, I guess," said Bert. "What do you think, John?"

"That could be done," said John, more enthusiastic now. "We could get working on it right away."

"I think you should wait until the big collision is past and see what happens here," I said. "We might not survive, after all."

They went off together chatting about the future. They seemed much more animated than when they came by. While I sat thinking things over, Marie and her brother-in-law, Dan, drove up. They, at least, were very pleased with everything.

"Peter has done us proud," said Marie. "He provided us with lots of plants. Mostly strawberries, raspberries and blueberries, but also a few black raspberries and three or four Saskatoon berry plants. I'd never even heard of those, but he says they're popular out west."

"I've heard of them," I said, "but I've never tasted one. You've accomplished a lot in a short time."

"The kids all helped where they could. Peter did the delicate stuff. Anyway, we're done."

"Besides the berries, he's also trusting us with various other types of fruit and a couple of cacao trees and coffee trees. I didn't know such things could grow here, but he's hopeful that it's warm enough. My wife is looking after the kids just now. She's pregnant, so I don't want her working too hard."

"Jimmy took one of the canoes out on the lake last night," said Marie, "and caught us a couple of large bass. I made him use a life jacket. He swims like a fish, but I don't want to risk anything. I thought I heard you say that the fish were okay to eat?"

"According to the scientists, they are perfectly fine. I'm excited about the prospect of harvesting our own coffee beans." I laughed. "I never thought I would be able to drink coffee again!"

As they walked toward the main camp, I spotted Dave, still busy digging latrines, so I wandered over to talk. Dave was in the middle of a short break, drinking coffee.

"How did you score a coffee?" I asked. "I thought it was to be rationed."

"Friends in high places, I guess," he said, smiling guiltily. "It will soon be only herbal tea, I suppose."

"Peter had the foresight to bring over a couple of coffee plants, so someday maybe we will have it again."

"Well, that would be the dream," he said. "I can't stomach herbal tea—I call it 'horrible' tea."

"How is the family?" I asked

"All well," he said. "Lots to do just now, anyway."

Once I left Dave, George found me, looking thoughtful.

"What should we do about petty crime?" he asked. "We have two or three families that continue to insist on taking more than their share."

"One thing we have plenty of is food," I replied. "I'd say let it go for now. We'll have a talk with them later. I think we should recruit the town police officers we have to carry on as our police force. You can be the head of security. Talk to the chief about it."

Mary, one of the astronomers, came out of what I liked to think of as the "command shack." It was, of course, just one of the Quonset huts that Bruce had taken over for his equipment. He now ran the gate functions from there, accompanied by several university types.

Mary said, "You're in charge of everyday affairs, correct? We need to tell all the people that they must stay outside during the next meteor strike—the big one—which, according to our best calculations, will occur in about six hours. They should all stay as far away from the gate as possible. We don't know what kind of backlash there will be. It's best to be as prudent as possible."

"I'll get the word out," I said. "Many of the people are far away at the moment, down to the south. I'll make sure they're told to stay where they are. Do you know anything more about this gate phenomenon yet? How it works, I mean? Have any of the people from the university said anything about it?"

"It's still more or less a complete mystery," she said. "We've narrowed it down a little, though. It appears to exhibit the properties of dark matter. The universe is mostly made up of dark matter, but we actually know very little about it. The gateway also appears to have something to do with magnetism, but again we can't be sure. There seems to be a particle involved that we haven't yet discovered but can theorize about. It's all just theory, but we have some very good minds working on it now."

I went in search of George and Raymond. I found Sue first. I asked her to spread the word that no one should be indoors when the big moment arrived, and that everyone should keep as far away from the gate as possible. I finally found George and passed on the same message to him. I asked him to get the town police to help with enforcement.

Albert arrived from the south to report that everyone down there was ready and waiting.

"The big event will be in about six hours," I said, "according to the best estimate. We need to have everyone outside during that time and keep everyone away from here. How is the food holding out?"

"No problem with food," he said. "We've got a huge surplus, even if people eat twice what they have been consuming. That group from PEI has already planted all the seed potatoes they had and has started on planting corn. They're a hard-working bunch."

Max Owens, the ex-real estate man, was sitting on a bench nearby, so I joined him for a cup of coffee. I was told to enjoy it as it would be my last cup for a while. The remaining coffee was being kept for special occasions.

"It looks as if you've made a lot of progress in laying out our new town," I said. "Are you finished already?"

"Not finished," he said. "I've got it well started. Thanks to you, that Quonset hut got moved. It slowed them down a bit in their building, but I think they found a better place for it. They were just spreading those things all over the place with little regard for the future. That first meteor strike scared the life out of many people, me included. I'll need another week or two to finish my plans. It will probably be in a state of flux for quite a while until things settle down. Any idea when you might get houses up?"

"The big problem is going to be building materials. We have some but nowhere near enough for all the houses we'll need."

"That's about how I had it figured, as well," he said. "We might get three or four out of what we have. There would be fights about who should get them. That was a good idea of yours to tell people that they would accumulate points toward houses by working hard. It sort of kills two birds with one stone."

"Let's hope it solves that problem, anyway," I said. "I'm sure people will find a fault with the system in time. They always do."

The next six hours dragged by with agonizing slowness. It seemed more like twice the time. Robert George and I moved our sleeping bags and possessions well up to the north. The rest of the people seemed to have done the same.

Finally, some violent tremors heralded the approaching shock. All of a sudden, there was an extremely heavy shock and flames shot out from the gate, blasting everything around it. Our hangar that we had worked so hard on lost most of its siding. The roof held, to my amazement. The Quonset hut that was to be the main dormitory slid sideways. The hut that housed the latrines fared better. It seemed to take the shock more from the side and moved very little. The office-cum-head-building shook violently and then settled back on the ground. Against all odds, the main gate held. Away over to the east, I saw a volcano erupt. Nothing like that happened nearby, but shock after shock kept things shaking. Luckily, they were not as severe as that first big one.

George grabbed Robert and me and we headed to the main building. The shocks were still coming but diminishing in intensity.

Inside the building, we discovered that two people had been injured, though not critically so. One had a broken leg and one had multiple bruises. Nobody had been killed, thank goodness, but everyone was incredibly shaken up. The doctor was busy stabilizing the broken leg when we got there. All those who had been in the building were hurting in one way or another.

I went back outside to where most people had ridden out the tremors. Two or three people were out cold and looked dead, but they had apparently just passed out. Others were screaming, and everyone was grouped around Reverend Stead. They were standing or sitting with their arms around each other. Many were praying. No one was badly hurt but many were bruised. The people who had been laid out on the ground began to recover. The doctor arrived and went to a man who was still lying down. The doctor said the man had had a heart attack. He was very weak.

By the time we'd walked back to the general population, my nerves had calmed down. It was still hard to walk a straight line as the aftershocks kept rattling around.

"I'd better see what has happened down in farming country," I said. "I'll take one of the jeeps. Do either of you wish to come with me?"

They both declined, as the aftershocks continued. I drove to the shallow ford in the river. Dan was there, having just returned from the main farms.

"How is everything and everybody out that way?" I asked

"Shook up a bit," said Dan, "but otherwise, no harm done. All the animals are still badly shaken. The cows, horses, sheep, and pigs went wild just before the main shock. Everybody is working hard to calm them. When might we hope these tremors will stop?"

"I've no idea," I replied. "Probably not for a few days."

"When the main shock hit, Betty, my wife, went into labour but it's far too soon. She calmed down quickly, and the pains quit coming; otherwise, I wouldn't have left her. I better get back, though, just in case."

"There's a doctor at the headquarters, if you need help."

"We'll be fine," he said.

"Don't risk it," I said. "Come get him if you need him."

I drove to Albert and Bonnie's place. They were out with the animals, trying to soothe shattered nerves. Dave and Leslie were there, as well. Everything looked to be under control. I drove on to John and Bert's. Racehorses are highly strung animals. Things looked to be total chaos. I got out of the jeep and went to the horses I knew best. They recognized me and calmed a little in my presence.

Dave was in the centre of four mares that were crowding around him. He was well known to the Toronto horses both by sight and by smell. They were calm because he was calm. Some were in a sweaty lather but were just standing, twitching and shaking. When I could see that the horses had calmed down a little, I got in the jeep and headed west to where our PEI folk had settled.

They were little more than shook up. They had been a long way from the gate and the shocks had not been as intense. They had their own prayer group gathered around and praying. They had almost a town of their own set up. At the four corners where their staked-out properties intersected, four families were grouped: one of the sheep ranchers, who had a host of children, one of the cattle farmers, and two separate PEI families. They had been busy planting and seemed happy enough. I told them of the devastation back at headquarters and that I would keep them up to date with any news as it happened.

I headed back to headquarters with the good news. All was well with our outlying friends and their properties. The same could not be said for the area near headquarters. There were many people bruised badly and a couple of broken limbs. The children were all pale and afraid. One man had been found dead, in addition to the heart-attack victim. Apparently, he had been in the hangar building. He had been warned but chose to ignore our advice.

"Do you know who this fellow was?" I asked George.

"A man from town. Some of the townsfolk have identified him," said George. "I guess he was asked several times to help at one project or another and then had skipped out after doing very little work. Nobody seemed to like him much. They thought he was nothing but a freeloader."

"Still, it's an innocent life lost," I said.

"It was a freak accident," said Robert. "The board that killed him came down end first and split his skull open. He would have been hurt by all the boards falling down on him, anyway, but this one just happened to catch him first."

"Who's the guy in the control building with the broken leg?" I asked.

"Apparently he's a theoretical mathematician," said George. "If anyone is going to find out what our friend Bruce has discovered here, it will be him. Robert and I were having breakfast near a couple of those university people and we heard them discussing some things. They are in agreement that the answer to all of this lies in what's called 'dark matter.' I had never even heard that term before, but they say the universe is mostly made up of this stuff. It sounds like there is a particle that they theorize is the cause behind all this."

"I've heard of dark matter," I said, "but I thought nothing was known about it because it can't be seen or detected."

"They said something about new particles being discovered all the time. They mentioned the newest one, calling it a 'Higgs boson,' but apparently that's ordinary matter and very small."

"At any rate," said Robert, "our hangar is a mess."

"That reminds me," I said. "I guess this falls in your area, George. Don't let anybody take the lumber. We must salvage all that we can of it. As for the hangar, it will need a lot of bracing before we can use it again."

Another tremor shook us gently as we talked, much lower in intensity than the earlier ones.

"We need to look at that new volcano over to the east," said Robert. "We can do a fly-by later today. All the aircraft came through the storm, or whatever you call it, quite well. They just got bounced around a little."

"I haven't eaten for a while," I said. "Let's see what's available then we can try flying out to the volcano. By the way, George, let the people eat all they want. They can be greedy if they like. We have lots of food."

"Okay," he said. "I'm against that sort of thing, but I'll try to be a little more relaxed about it."

By the time we finished eating, a big thunderstorm had started up, so we took shelter until it had passed us.

"What's going on with this weather?" asked George. "I thought we didn't get thunderstorms here."

"It's probably due to all the seismic activity from the meteor strike," said Robert, "and perhaps that volcano over there. We'll do a thorough preflight check before we fly over to see it. Ron, you come with me and George can stand by with one of the Cessna 150s as our back-up."

"Okay," said George. "A 150 is more my style, anyway."

In a short while, the thunderstorm blew itself off to the south so Robert and I both did a very thorough preflight check, each doing it separately. Nothing was out of place; the plane had taken a shaking, nothing more.

The volcano was at the farthest reaches of the area we had previously mapped. It wasn't large. We didn't go very near, just observed from a distance of about five miles. That was close enough for me. There was a steady rain falling near it; hopefully that would cool things down.

Just to be sure all was well with the farms, we flew low and slow past each one. We were waved at when we got near all of them. There was general peace and quiet descending. We landed and went to the headquarters to pass on our observances.

"Keep up the good work," said Bruce. "I'm still getting tremors from Earth. Two Moons, as far as I can tell, has settled down nicely. We've been very lucky."

I reported how we were set up organization-wise; he was pleased and asked us to keep on working together and not bother to report back to him about every little detail. He felt we were headed in the right direction and he was going to be busy with the theory of this place. He asked me to continue to run things, as he was impressed at how we were managing. I was just glad to be able to help out.

CHAPTER 15

At the end of three weeks' time, things were settling into a routine. It seemed like everyone had accepted that life as we knew it on Earth was over. Reverend Stead said that tomorrow was Sunday, and he would hold a service. We had built a stage to talk to the people. Reverend Stead had been busy the past three weeks talking to many people. Tomorrow would be his first Sunday service here on Two Moons. Almost the whole of our population had said they were going to come to it. How everybody was going to hear anything was a mystery.

The rumour around was that Dave's older brother, Raymond Gransden, and his family were supplying the music for the service. I was not surprised as Raymond and family had played the music at our church back in Peterborough several times and often played and sang at the nursing home there. I was surprised when they came to set up around nine o'clock to see that they had brought their sound equipment with them.

They had several microphones, as well as a couple of speakers. They set up the generator to supply electricity. They also had a small upright piano. How they got the piano over in the last-minute scramble was anyone's guess.

A crowd started gathering early on; shortly after, the Gransdens started to set up. A contingent of people from the PEI crowd arrived. They had the farthest to come. They had brought their friend the shepherd and some of his family with them. I said hello to Peter and family. He asked me about the Gransden family and I told him to just listen, he would be surprised. By ten o'clock, the time the service was to start, the area was crowded with most of the population of Two Moons.

Reverend Stead came up to the main microphone and opened with a word of prayer. When he had finished, nine-year-old Susan Gransden stepped up to the microphone and started to play "Amazing Grace" on her violin. When she finished the first verse, the rest of the family joined in. Her mother played the piano, and the rest of the family each played a violin. It was an impressive sight, five violins in a row. The only one left out was their toddler. When they finished there was thunderous applause. The enthusiasm of the crowd astounded me.

Bob, their thirteen-year-old son, and Gene, who was six, came forward with their mother and father. Sheila took her mother's place at the piano and Susan picked up an accordion during the applause, and when the crowd had settled, mom, dad, Bob and Gene sang, "Because he Lives" and again there was loud applause. They harmonized beautifully.

The reading from the Bible followed. It was from the 46th Psalm in the Old Testament. Reverend Stead then came to the microphone to deliver the message. He spoke of hope: "God is our refuge and strength, a very present help in our trouble." This verse spoke of the ever-present hope we needed to have in God. He wound up a half hour later quoting from Isaiah 43: "When you pass through the waters, I will be with you."

You could have heard a pin drop even in that large crowd. They were thinking about what they had heard and where they now found themselves.

After the sermon, Mrs. Gransden sang "How Great Thou Art." She had a beautiful strong soprano voice. On the last high note, she held it for what seemed an impossibly long time. Then Raymond joined his wife on stage, and Sheila sat back down at the piano to accompany her mom and dad as they sang "Just a Closer walk With Thee." Reverend Stead ended the service with a prayer. He particularly prayed for a woman who had lost her sanity during the meteor strike. She had been wandering around the compound all day and night talking, but no one could understand what she was saying.

George came on the microphone next and said that he wanted to give folks a bulletin on the state of things. He told them we had lots of food and wouldn't be running out. He asked them not to be greedy and to listen to the supervisors and then told them of the work-for-credits pay system and how the construction of houses were going to start soon and would be allotted by accumulated credit standing.

The service had gone very well. Many people commented to me how much they liked it. They felt more at peace with things after being here today. The service was followed by a roast beef lunch. It almost felt like home on a Sunday. After lunch while I was finishing a cup of tea, I was approached by a woman whom I had seen around but whose name I did not know.

"I'm Debbie Colander," she said. "I understand you're running things now. I wondered if you would mind if my friends and I set up an amateur acting group. We had a group in Smith's Falls, but only about three of us are here. I have a few comedies—plays—that we could put on as entertainment."

“I think that would be a super idea,” I said. “You noticed how well the Gransdens were received just now.”

“Yes, I did,” she replied. “That’s what got me to thinking. We’ll have to recruit a few others—there are more parts than the few of us can play by ourselves.”

“Go ahead and do what you need,” I said. “If you need any help with building props or that sort of thing, let me know and I’ll see what can be done.”

“Thank you,” she said in departure. “I’ll let you know how it goes.”

As she left, I almost got pounced on by Mike and Max Owens. I saw that Mike was turning out to be much more than just a DC3 mechanic. They had been waiting to catch me free of other distractions.

“We’ve been talking about housing,” said Max. “The people are reasonably content just now but want to know when we might get started on construction.”

“Once a real estate agent,” I replied, “always a real estate agent, I guess.”

“Mike here thinks we can make bricks to build the houses. He knows how to make concrete. What we need is some limestone. Do you know if there is some nearby?”

“I think I know where there is a deposit in the hills over there. I’ve never been near the place, but I’ve seen it from the air. We can have it tested easily enough.”

“The ancient cement made by the Egyptians for their pyramids and later referred to as ‘Roman cement’ is pretty easy to make,” said Mike. “Dave’s going to let us use that mixer he got from the rental agency back on Earth. We have very little lumber so the houses will need to be all brick.”

"We'll need to start them soon, I guess," I said. "People will feel better if they see we're moving toward constructing more permanent dwellings. The accommodations in the Quonset huts are okay for now, but people can be picky."

"Mike and I would like to start an industry suppling bricks for houses and things," said Max. "We know where there is plenty of nice fine sand. Even if we hire some people to help, it will still take several days to make bricks for each house."

"Sounds like a good start-up industry, but to avoid later conflict you should talk to my son James. He was a lawyer back on Earth."

"Good idea," said Max.

The remainder of the day was a nice quiet day of feasting and celebrating that we were alive. Later in the afternoon, the Gransdens took another turn on the stage and promised further shows to come. Everyone stayed up late and went to bed tired, vowing to get to work at various tasks starting tomorrow.

Albert and Bonnie, being farm folk, were up early. They were going to start a sort of farm co-op to supply the people with food. They wanted to know who they could get to run a store to distribute the food. I gave them the names of a few people who were anxious to help but didn't know what they should volunteer for. Albert mentioned that we should also set up an abattoir for the slaughter of animals. Another thing for me to think about.

I seemed to be endlessly busy talking to people. George came storming up with the ex-police chief from town. "We just found out a young girl was attacked last night here on Two Moons," said George. "It took a while to get the story from her. Her parents are fuming."

"What happened?" I asked. "And when?"

"She was out late," said William, the police chief. "She was almost back to the dormitory where she usually sleeps near her mother when she was grabbed from behind. She put up a fight and says she scratched him on the side of his neck. She ran for the dormitory and managed to get inside but didn't tell her mother until this morning."

"Did she get a look at him?" I asked. "We don't have as many people here on Two Moons, so we should be able to figure out who it is."

"I think I know who it is," George said somberly.

"You do?" I said. "What—Who is it?"

"There have been clues all along. I just wasn't following the first rule of being a good investigator which is not to exclude anyone. Ron, could you get Frank, our aircraft mechanic? Bring him here to see us."

Speechless, unable to believe Frank could be our man, I simply nodded and went to look for him. When we came back, George said, "Frank can you roll down the collar on your turtleneck for us?"

"I'd rather not," said Frank. "It's kind of cool out today. What's the problem?"

"Get out of the jeep and roll down your collar or you can take the turtleneck completely off, if you like. I think you are our rapist. Melinda scratched you last night. I've seen you before, after the attacks in town, with cuts or scratches on your body. You also use the same matches that I found at the original attack site, where you killed your cousin."

Frank reached under the seat of the jeep and came up with a gun, which he pointed at William, then George and me. "I'm just going to drive away. If I can do that, without you busybodies interfering, then nobody will be hurt," he said and started the jeep.

I stood there with my mouth open, not knowing what to do. He hadn't confessed, but it appeared that George was right. Frank peeled out and headed north at a fast pace. Finally, I got it together and asked William if he had a gun.

"Not on me," he said. "I can get it, though."

"Be quick about it," I said. "I'll get a plane ready. Come meet me on the runway as soon as you can with your gun. We can catch him. It's open country out there."

"George," I said, "get a manhunt underway. Get Robert in the air as soon as you locate him. I'll keep in touch on the radio."

I did a quick preflight, then started the plane. It was another five minutes or so before William returned. He had a rifle, as well as his sidearm. When he had his seatbelt on, I gunned it and did a short field take-off.

"Don't undo your seatbelt," I said. "The window slides open; you can shoot out that."

William looked white as a sheet. "I've never flown before," he said. "I feel kind of sick."

"There's nothing to worry about," I replied. "If you have to throw up, there's a bag under the seat. He only has a ten- or fifteen-minute start on us. I don't see him yet."

I was flying low at almost full speed. I had only cut back slightly on the throttle.

"I'm going to climb up to get a longer view," I said. "That should help us see where he went."

William was looking a little green around the gills, but he was enduring it fine. I was now farther north than I had ever been before, but there was still no sign of him. The hills back where we lived had disappeared from view. How had Frank managed to get away? New, higher hills came up to the east of us, but still no sign of Frank or the jeep.

"He must have turned east," I said to William. "I'm turning around. We'll go back to the valley or pass and go east from there. He must have a destination in mind."

Robert called on the radio. He was airborne in a DC3. He had one of the other police officers with him. There was a sliding window at the copilot position. That was where his companion could shoot from, if needed. I told him I thought Frank had turned east, and that I was headed through the gap eastward.

"I have you in my sights," he replied. "You're above me and to the east and north a bit. I'll fly a more southerly route than you; that way we can cover more ground. Holler if you spot him."

We flew back and forth for three hours, joined by one of the 150s mid-search. We found nothing and were forced to return to base. George had meanwhile organized a ground search, commandeering all the available vehicles. The day passed. Nothing, not even a trace of Frank was found. He must have gone to ground somewhere, but where was the big question.

During the night, a large quantity of our fuel disappeared. Clearly Frank was nearby. Some food had disappeared, as well. He was the boldest fugitive there ever was. We continued our air and ground search for three days with no results. He had completely vanished. There were some signs of where a jeep had been driven but whether it was him or just one of our searchers was unknown. Then fuel and food disappeared from Albert and Bonnie's farm overnight. Two more worrisome days went by.

Mid-morning the next day, Joe Smythe, one of our sheep men, came skidding into the main compound. His herd was out west past Peter Wright's—our PEI friend's—compound. He was very excited. "I saw him," he exclaimed as he jumped out of his car. "He's slaughtering one of my sheep right now on the extreme west of where I have my herd."

"Did you frighten him off?" I asked.

"I don't think so," he replied. "I don't think he even heard me drive away. I didn't hear him or the shot that killed the sheep. Too far away from where I was. The sheep were clustered around where we were, and I wondered why, so I got my binoculars and there he was, bold as brass. I didn't know whether my old car would start—I haven't used it since we got here. I haven't converted it yet to that new fancy fuel you're using. She got me here, though."

I yelled for George, Richard, and everyone to come. I grabbed William, and we took off in the 180. We were first to take off, but Richard and another police officer were close behind. George was starting up another plane and some of the men were climbing into jeeps. I kept the 180 going at its best speed while I climbed to 5000 feet. We could see a long way from that height.

Frank was indeed not far from the western edge of the flock. He was driving very fast. We had him. He couldn't escape this time.

Robert, flying a DC3, came up on my left. I cautioned him to stay a distance away. Frank likely still had his gun. William stuck his rifle out the window and took a shot at the jeep, aiming for the tires.

"Save your ammunition!" I yelled. "We're almost a mile from him and he's going too fast. We need to get closer. Be ready."

George somehow had caught up to us in the 150. *He must have the throttle wide open*, I thought. As he drew up to us, I asked who he had with him. I could see two people but was unable to name them. He replied that he had Jimmy and Dan, Jimmy's uncle, both armed with rifles. They were both very good shots. He was below us. I saw a rifle go off from one of the windows and a tire immediately blew out. The jeep lost control and started to roll. Frank was thrown out of it.

George was lowest and landed first. It took a while for Robert and me to descend, but we, too, landed nearby. Frank was unconscious but still alive. We loaded him into the DC3 and headed for home. We had our guy. We could salvage the jeep later if it was worthwhile.

When we got to the main compound, the doctor came forward to examine Frank. He was in bad shape. We had not bothered taking care in how we handled him getting him into the DC3. We told the doctor to just let him die. He was a murderer. The doctor's training wouldn't allow him to do that. The patient was still alive. He had Frank put on a stretcher and taken into a Quonset hut. Most of the crowd wanted him dead. But in the end, William prevailed.

"There must be a trial," he maintained.

It turned out that Dan was the shooter. William took statements from every one of us who had been involved. I reflected how Jimmy had stood up to that bear a few short weeks ago. It could have easily been him who had shot the tire out. I was glad it wasn't his shot. I didn't want to see him be accused of killing someone. He had seen his own father killed by a madman when he was very young.

CHAPTER 16

Frank was in poor shape. He had many broken bones and was barely alive. A cot was placed in the rear corner of the Quonset hut we had been using as the headquarters. It was open to the rest of the building, but we got some men to start bricking up a large cell. A guard was placed on him. In my opinion, I didn't think he was going anywhere. All he did was lie there and moan.

The doctor didn't give him anything for the pain. That was approved of by most of the population. A large portion of the people wanted to just kill him. I guess that was the guard's main purpose, to see that nobody did kill him. We had set up a daily briefing to tell the people what news there was. We told them that if Frank recovered there would be a trial. I had been given a box-like structure to serve as a desk in that hut. It was a popular hangout.

I needed a secretary to keep people at a distance so I could see one person at a time. One of our builder friends said he would build me a separate office to allow me to get away a little. He put a couple of men to work at it.

Mike and Max came first. They wanted to know if a source of limestone had been found. I informed them that it had but I didn't know just where it was. They wanted permission to start to make bricks. They wanted something in writing so they could show people that was what they were doing to help get houses built. I wrote them a short note and told them my son the lawyer would write up a more permanent agreement. I sent them to Bruce to ask if he knew where the rock was to be found. Many people crowded around asking if I knew what was going to happen to Frank. I told them that I didn't know. They kept asking. I had to get away from that, so I got in a jeep and headed south. I went to see my Chapleau friends. Marie met me as I drove up.

"To what do we owe this pleasant surprise?" said Marie." You don't usually come by. Would you like a cup of tea and a cookie?"

"That would hit the spot," I said. "I had to get away from all the questions about Frank. Are you here by yourself?"

"Well, everyone is around somewhere. Dan is with Betty; she's close to having the baby. She generally stays inside these days. Jimmy is fishing, I think. He catches quite a few fish. He says there are lots and they are eager to bite just about anything. The other kids are out playing somewhere—a couple of them have taken to gardening in a big way."

"You know we have a doctor here and Leslie is a veterinarian. She could help with Betty's delivery. I think we may even have a nurse or two amongst us."

"We'll let you know if she has difficulty, but I had all of my kids at home with little help. We'll manage."

"No need to bravely soldier on alone," I said. "Might as well get help. People need to feel they have a purpose."

"I think she has another week or so left," she replied, "but it's comforting to know help is near."

"I keep meaning to come down and do a little fishing to relax," I said. "Maybe you could send Jimmy up to bring my boat down to your dock. I'll fix a time to go out with him when he comes for it."

"I'm sure he'd love that. I'll ask him when he comes back."

"Great! Well, I think I'll go see how Dave, Leslie and family are doing."

"See you soon," she said as I drove off.

When I got to the shallow ford, Dave and Leslie were in the water on the other side. They were in their clothes and soaking wet, splashing each other and laughing uproariously.

"What's so funny?" I asked. "I could use a good laugh."

"It's nothing really," said Leslie. "We were just celebrating. That farmer over there"—she said, pointing to one of the original farms—"he's a grumpy standoffish type. He called me over today. One of his cows was having a hard time giving birth. She was exhausted when I got there. I think she must have been in labour for over an hour. She was going to die if I didn't do something.

"The farmer was trying to prove that I was no good as a vet. When I got down and put my arm inside the cow, I found out right away it was a breech. The calf's head was back and over his right shoulder. The farmer knew what the problem was and kept saying that I'd have to cut the calf up into pieces and get it out that way. He thought the calf was dead. That's all he knew. If the calf had been dead, that is exactly what I would have done to save the mother's life. But when I got my hand in there, the calf's tongue twitched, so I knew it wasn't dead yet—just stuck. Every time I tried to push it back, the cow had another contraction and pushed the calf harder against my arm. I tried to get a rope on the calf's head, but my arms weren't long enough so I yelled for Dave. He finally got the rope over its head. I told him to push back hard and I pulled the head around with the rope. The calf's head finally dropped onto its front legs and next contraction he slid right out.

"The poor cow was spent—she didn't even try to get up. The calf was blue in the face from lack of oxygen, but when we cleared its mouth, it started to breathe. We put him up near his mama's face, and when she sniffed him, she made an effort to rise. As soon as she licked him a little, they both came around fast. The dumb farmer kept saying he had never seen anything like that.

"Anyway, after all that, we were kind of messy, so we came over here to wash off. I'm glad it worked out. If I had to cut the beast out in pieces, we would have been a lot messier what with all the blood and guts there would have been. Can you give us a ride home? We need to change."

After dropping Dave and Leslie off, I continued on to see how the horses were getting on in their new surroundings. John and Will were standing chatting with Bert Mason.

"I can't see what use the horses are anymore," said Will. "There is no racing industry here."

"We'll just have to make one then," I said. "Entertainment is always needed. We no doubt will be slow to get there, but we will."

"We've kept the horses in training," said John, "but we'll have to build a training track. Do you have any plans for doing that in the future?"

"Mostly vague ideas," I replied. "I'd ideally like to see a track up near the main settlement with races maybe twice a month, initially. Then later, say, once a week. We have a bit of a grandstand now. We could build a better one at the track with seating on the other side. I haven't talked to anyone else about the idea, but I think it would be accepted."

"We can set up a track here for training as a start," said Bert, "then use that experience to get a bigger one back at the main area. The main problem I see is we have little or no lumber for railings. The horses are used to that as a guide."

"Do you have any of that bamboo stuff growing around here?" I asked. "Maybe it could be used as posts and rails. It would not need to be very sturdy and that bamboo grows fast."

"That's a good idea," said John. "There is a large stand of it out to the west. We will get some to try later today. By the way, I had to get Leslie to operate on Kingston Kenny. He got a bad case of colic. I thought he would die, but she cut him open and straightened his gut out. She did a neat job of it, as well."

"I'm glad she could help. It's great to have a veterinarian around. We have a lot of animals here."

I made Peter Wright and our Prince Edward Island people my last visit of the day. All was well in their world. I told them about Leslie's recent interventions; they already knew of the horse with colic.

While we were eating supper, I asked several people to join me in a meeting after the meal. When we were all gathered, I said, "Thanks for coming, Bruce asked me to sort of run things. I think it's time we sorted out a few things and got a little more organized. I don't mind running the show for now. But there are questions that I shouldn't decide alone. For instance, we need a sort of judicial council to decide what to do about Frank.

"Then we need a person to issue approvals to start up businesses. We have a couple going already. Mike and Max are setting up a brick-making business, for example. What do we do with the bricks?"

"That's easy," said George, "we build houses."

"What about administration buildings and things like a viewing stand for a racetrack, if John and Max get one set up? There are many other uses. But we need to set guidelines for what the bricks can be used for. We need to know how many houses we need to build and where they should go and who is to get them when they are completed.

"I don't mind setting up these planning meetings. I do think we should have at least one a week for a while. Mary, our lead astronomer, probably needs bricks as well as workers to set up her observatory. We really should know what direction to take and from whom.

"Then we have the question of what to do with the children. There are about forty or fifty of them. They should be educated. Do you want me to set up something for that? I used to be a teacher and a principal. I can start by mentioning these things in our morning briefing to the population, tomorrow."

The general consensus was that these things should all go ahead. After breakfast the next morning I made my announcements and then I got together with George, William, and my son James.

I opened the meeting by stating the obvious. We needed some official way to deal with Frank.

"I don't think we have enough of a population or any need for a jury of twelve good men," I said, "but we need to make it as official as we can. I think the best way for now is to have a set of judges. I would suggest three would be right. These should be appointed for now, maybe to sit for a year. We don't have a lot of crime, but that doesn't mean we won't have crime of some sort. These judges should be as representative as possible and should eventually be elected. One from farm folk, one from town folk and maybe one from business. George you used to be police. Would you sit as head judge for now?"

"I would," said George, "but what about William here?"

"I was thinking of appointing William as prosecutor for now, because he knew the folks in Smith's Falls and could best do that job. I thought that James could act as defence attorney. Do you guys think you could do those things? If not, is there anyone you would suggest?"

"I'm okay with it," said William.

My son nodded his agreement. "Who would be the other judges?"

"I was thinking of Max Owens for one and Marie Richardson from Chapleau for the other. I think we should have four who can act in that role but three will do for now. We can appoint someone else later."

"Why Marie?" said George.

"Two reasons," I said. "First we need both sexes represented, and she doesn't come from around here. Second, her husband was murdered so she will have empathy for the families. I don't have any idea how Marie or Max feel about capital punishment. I don't know if that matters, but we can ask them if you like."

"That's probably as fair as we're going to be able to make it," said George. "Is there anything else we should talk about at the moment?"

"Not that I can think of," I said. "Go away and think it over and let me know tomorrow what you think."

"How can I defend someone who is obviously guilty?" asked James.

"I know you specialize in real estate law," I said. "I'm not going to set up your defence for you, but you have a brain. Use it."

I had two people waiting to talk to me about teaching at the school. They couldn't have been more of a contrast. One woman was about fifty years old, and the other in her late teens.

"I really must get an office of some kind built," I said. "Which of you is up first?"

"I'm Mrs. Westbrook, Hannah," said the older of them. "I guess I was here first, but you can take us in any order you like."

"Please take Mrs. Westbrook first," said the teen. "I've never been a teacher before, but I'd like to talk about the job. I would like to teach if you'll have me."

"What's your name?" I asked. "Please sit over there and I'll get to you as soon as I can."

"My name is Jane Scofield," she said. "Thank you for seeing me."

Once Jane had taken a seat, I turned to Mrs. Westbrook. "Have you taught school before?"

"Yes, since I was twenty-one. I started teaching grade one and have taught several grades over the course of my career."

"I was a teacher most of my life, as well," I said, "then I served in the war. I haven't taught since. Would you be interested in leading the way, with help from myself to see what we can do for our young people?"

"I would like that," she said. "How do you propose we start?"

"I think we need a total of four or five teachers, some men and some women. We can talk about what to teach later, but I'd like to see academic subjects plus sports and help for the young teens in deciding what they want to do in life, with mentorship by our adult workers. Do you think you could you work with a rookie like Jane over there?"

"I'd love to work with her. Call her over and we'll talk together; she's a nice, polite young woman."

"As of this minute, you two are our schoolteachers," I said. "We will add more teachers as we go along. What I'd like you to do for now is to set up a few lessons for the very young. For example, basic reading and mathematics, as well as printing and so on. We can talk later about more advanced subjects later. I'll set out to look for more teachers, but if you know anybody who would be interested in the job, tell them to see me, or tell me and I will go see them."

Sue was next on my list. I needed her or someone she knew to be a secretary for me. I was also curious to see how her inventory of the population we had on Two Moons was coming along.

When I found her, I asked her, "Sue, have you completed the list of all the people here on Two Moons yet?"

"Yes, all done," she said, "and that includes the newborns."

"I need you to ask all those people what skills they have. Not just what they did for a living, but everything they know how to do. For example, our clothes are going to wear out on us. We need to be able to replace them. We will have wool from our sheep so we can make yarn. Find out if there is anyone who can use a spinning wheel. Find out who can tan leather or make it into belts, purses and so on. Anybody who does crafts of any sort. Do you understand?"

"Yes, I understand," she said. "It's going to take a while, though, with all our people out working on this or that."

"Yes, it will. If you need more people to help, recruit them. We need this list as soon as possible."

I got in the jeep and drove out to the farms. I told all the farmers that we needed all the skins from all the animals that were slaughtered for food. I asked the sheep farmers to bring the wool to me once their sheep had been sheared. I even made sure that the horse people knew that if a horse died, we needed their hide for manufacturing purposes, as well as the meat for dog food. I enjoyed my time driving around. I had been feeling very desk-bound, but somebody had to do my job.

CHAPTER 17

Max and Mike, our brick men, came in the office. They wanted to know the limits of their business concerns and how they should proceed.

"If you're worried about using the limestone or sand or whatever, then don't be. I'll get my son to give you a permit to use all that and the land it stands on."

"We want to build a kiln to roast the limestone," said Mike. "We can just use granite or whatever native rock there is to build the kiln. There is a large hill that's just pure sand near the limestone. We need to know about hiring staff and how we pay them and how the bricks will be paid for."

"At the moment, I'm the planetary representative" I said. "The bricks come to my possession as the local government. I will decide how the bricks get allotted. Some will go to building houses and some to government buildings. For instance, we need a mill built by the waterfall for grinding flour and corn and for power production, if we can manage to get it going. The generators won't last forever. So, make us some blocks as well as bricks. I would like to see you get production up to around a thousand bricks a day. You will need men to work for you; hire some. For now, you can use one jeep and the flatbed army truck. If you need anything else, just ask."

"That's what we wanted to know," said Max. "I'm sure we'll have other questions soon, but for now this is great."

"Max, I need to ask you if you would serve as a judge on a panel of three judges to try Frank's case. Eventually, that's how we'll settle legal issues. The position will be elective, but at the moment we can't wait for an election. I need to know your answer by the end of the week. That will give you a little time to think about it."

"I don't know anything about legal things," said Max, "but I'm happy to help any way I can."

"You don't need to know anything; George will show you what you need to do."

"Okay, I'll let you know soon."

I was unsure how many bricks we needed for a house, but after thinking it over and considering the size of bricks, I thought we would need 10,000 to 15,000 bricks per house. The houses had to be solid brick. We had very little wood for framing.

I was relaxing with a cup of tea when John, my former racehorse trainer, came in to see about a place for a track near town that could be used for entertainment.

"We got a track set up for training the horses," said John. "That bamboo idea for the rails has worked well. The horses see it and it gives them guidance, but if they bump it the bamboo just breaks and doesn't hurt the horse."

"The perfect solution by the sound of things," I said. "Any thoughts on where we should put a track here for entertaining the people?"

"As close as possible to where the houses will be," he said. "They shouldn't have far to walk to get there. I like a one-mile track. That will have only two turns. Better for the horses."

"We're kind of limited as to where to put the track," I said. "To the south, we have the sewage plant. To the west is the river. To the east is mountainous. So, it must be the land to the north between the river and the mountains. Let's go see how it looks on the ground."

"It needs to be about three quarters of a mile from end to end and a little over half a mile wide. That way the turns are not too sharp. We need an area at the rear, toward the mountains, I guess, to have a backstretch, where the horses get harnessed and stabled before racing.

"We could put the spectator stands on the side toward the lake, with their back to the lake. That would put the performing stage in the middle of the track. We need to keep the track as far back from the lake as possible for safety."

We agreed on this spot as the best available. John headed home to get his men and get started on the track here at the main base. It was exciting to think that very soon we would be able to see our horses compete again.

Marie was working out in the fields when I dropped by. I didn't realize until then the extent of berries and fruit that had been planted. When they all came into fruit, we would be buried in them.

"Hi, Marie! How are things with you and yours?" I asked. "And where is everyone?"

"The younger kids are out fishing," she said. "Betty is over there working with the few bushes we have. She has her infant with her. Dan went over to Dave's place; Jimmy is up in the mountains in back of here. He found a lake up there with a stream coming down into the lake. He thinks he can divert enough of the water our way to give us running water like we had back home. He gets more like his father every day. They'll all be back soon for lunch."

Dan came into the yard as we were talking. "Nice to see you," he said. "I was helping Dave put up new wire for another pasture for his cattle. How are things in town?"

"Things are proceeding well," I replied. "I need to ask Marie here if she would act on a panel of three judges to try Frank's case. George will be the lead; he can show you what you need to know. We'll eventually hold an election for these positions, but for now I'm appointing—provided you'll do it?"

"I think the answer is yes," said Marie, "but I'll give you a definite answer after I think it over."

"That's perfect," I said. "I just need to know by the end of the week. Dan, you know how to tan hides don't you? We need to start saving our resources. Can you set up a business doing that?"

"Yes, we can do that. Jimmy is a good hand at it, as well."

"Dan," I said, "could you or Jimmy take me and maybe George and Robert out for a little fishing this evening? We need a little break from the routine, and fish for supper would be great for a change."

"We'd love to," said Dan.

"Well, I'd better get back to town," I said wearily. "The people can't seem to get along without playing twenty questions all the time. It seems I'm the only person able to answer."

I drove back to the main camp. I loved the quiet time to think. It turned out to be a quiet day; most people had found something to occupy their time. Robert and I ended up going fishing. George's time was taken up with researching his new judicial role.

We split up in two boats: Robert with Dan in one, and me with Jimmy in the other boat. Both boats kept close to shore.

"Does the water get rough out farther in the lake?" I asked Jimmy. "Or is the fishing better in the shallower water?"

"I've never seen the water as rough as it used to get on the lake back home," said Jimmy thoughtfully, "and I've never tried fishing way out. There doesn't seem to be any need unless there are much bigger fish out there. Whether they're bigger out there I don't know. I guess they would be."

"How big are the bass you've caught?" I asked. "And have you caught any pickerel or muskies in here?"

"The bass are typically three to four pounds and the pickerel are six or seven, with the odd one bigger than that," he replied. "I've only caught one muskie, but I haven't tried too hard. The muskie was about fifteen pounds. What would you like to try for?"

"Bass will be fine. If we catch a pickerel, that would be great. I just want a fish for supper. I'm tired of all the beef, pork and mutton."

The fish didn't seem to care what kind of bait was used. They were just hungry. We kept a few larger ones but also released many. The fish were eager, but we had no need of so many.

Robert had caught several, as well. We took what we could use and went back to the base. Before we left, I told Dan and Jimmy they should offer fishing excursions. Many people in town would shell out credits to do what we just experienced.

Robert and I got out of the jeep near our bedroll and fire. George was already there. He had a harried look on his face. There was an older couple passing by.

"You've been fishing," the man said. "I didn't know there were fish here."

"I love fish," his companion added. "We should have brought our fishing tackle."

"Hello," I said, "we haven't been introduced. My name is Ron Withers. Bruce introduced the fish years ago. They haven't spread everywhere yet, but they are catchable."

"Our names are Cathy and Rick Norton," he said. "I'm afraid we haven't been able to make ourselves of much avail. I'm unable to lift or work hard. We were retired back in Smith's Falls. Fishing was about all we did before we came here."

"There's lots of fish here. Why don't you come over for supper at my place? Or maybe you only like catching and not so much eating fish?"

"Oh, gosh no," said Cathy. "Fish is our favourite food, but we don't want to intrude."

"We'd love to have company," I said. "What did you do for a living before you retired?" I asked. "I was a schoolteacher."

"We were both geologists, looking for different types of rock and things," said Rick, "but we taught a little, as well."

"Would you like to teach our young people about geology? We need to pass our skills down to our young folk."

"You might say we loved our work," said Cathy enthusiastically. "For me, the answer is a definite yes."

"That's great to hear," I said. "As to fishing, you can borrow my tackle and I'll see that you will be able to use the raft over there."

The fish was delicious as only fresh caught fish can be. The Nortons made very good dinner guests. When they left, I turned to George and said, "You look like you have the weight of the world on your shoulders. What's worrying you, my friend?"

"It's Frank. I didn't think there would be much to a trial. The biggest problem is there are two distinct patterns of thought in action. Numerous times a day, I get someone's sincere advice that we should execute Frank immediately. Then someone else joins in with a staunch opinion against capital punishment. The people are about split: half one way, half the other. All of them feel totally sure they are right and the other side wrong. Everyone knows he's guilty, but what do we do about it? That's the dilemma."

"Personally," I said, "I'm for execution, but how about castration or maybe a frontal lobotomy? That might satisfy both groups. Castration is supposed to make a man less aggressive and uninterested in sex. I have, however, heard that one's sex drive sometimes remains, but the person is unable to perform. That would be very frustrating, I should think, and could lead to violent action. If that happened, then the frontal lobotomy would be all that's left. Then you would still have a live person, but a total vegetable."

"Thanks," said George, "you've given me some things to think about. You always have a way of seeing all sides of things."

Three days later, Sue got back to me with a complete list of everyone's skills and hobbies. The list was long and impressive. I called the teachers in for a talk and they brought along a young man who was introduced as a prospect. His name was Don Cameron.

I brought out Sue's list and said, "We have a list here showing all the children under fifteen years old. There are forty-seven of them altogether; ten are between five and eight years old, twelve are between nine and eleven, and another twelve are between twelve and fifteen. The remainder are under five years old. My suggestion is that one of you take the five- to eight-year-olds and start them on letters and numbers, just basic things. Someone else can take the nine-to-eleven-age children and do reading, math and more advanced things. The older kids can be given to a couple I just met, Cathy and Rick Norton. They are retired geologists and are looking for some way to contribute. They can take the kids and teach them about geology and go on field trips to do practical lessons. I will find other professionals to teach about other practical subjects, from animal husbandry to carpentry to cement-making. I think we also need at least one day a week for recreation, like soccer or baseball. Track and field would be good, or maybe indoor games. If you need my help with any of this, just ask."

They sat in a corner of the hut for a long time, talking and planning. Hannah came by later to say that they had come up with a schedule and would keep me posted on their efforts. A couple of ladies had set up a tea room in the corner of our building. My carpenter had nearly finished the construction of my private office beside it, as well. Things were progressing nicely.

The women from the tea shop were serving herbal teas and had baked biscuits, squares and rolls, in addition to small cakes and fruit pies. A veritable bonanza.

Dan and Jimmy came to see me. Jimmy wondered if he could borrow a stone hammer. He said he had found a lake up in the mountains behind their property. He wanted to divert the stream to give them running water like they had at their old home.

"Certainly, you may borrow a stone hammer," I said. "Do you need any help breaking the rock?"

"No," said Dan, "I don't think so. We only need to divert a small bit of the flow. The remainder would still go down the mountain into the lake. The part we would divert would wind up in the lake, as well, after we used it for washing and drinking and so on."

"Running water is a big problem out here," I said. "After you complete your work, maybe you could show the other farmers what you did."

"We'd be glad to do that," said Jimmy. "Those people there are very nice."

The doctor came by to say that Frank was fit enough to stand trial. I alerted the members of the judicial committee and our appointed lawyers. My son James said he was as ready as he would ever get. I gave them three days and informed everyone the next morning at our daily briefing of the decision to begin the legal proceedings.

The court date arrived without fanfare. A huge crowd, almost everyone on the planet, gathered to watch. The judges were supplied with a desk and chairs on the platform we used for delivering news bulletins and church services.

George banged on the table with a gavel to show that he wanted people to hear what he was going to say. He then spoke of how it had been decided to use three people to judge crimes, and how we were starting with the three people now on the stage. He said that eventually there would be four, in case someone took ill or something of the sort when a trial was needed. The four would eventually be elected, and in the future there would be elections for many positions in the community. This matter, however, was too pressing to wait that long. George sat down and called for Frank and James, Frank's defence attorney, to come forward.

Marie read out the charges that they had prepared and asked Frank how he pleaded to the charges. Frank didn't hesitate; he just replied, "Guilty." Some people in the crowd started yelling to execute him. George had to bang to on the table long and hard for there to be a semblance of quiet. The people who were against capital punishment had been yelling, as well. A couple of fights broke out and our small police force did the best they could to calm things and restore order. George warned everyone that if they created a disturbance, they would be charged and fined an amount of credits to be determined.

When quiet was restored, George said, "Mr. Howard, you must see yourself that we cannot allow someone in our community to be raping and murdering our citizens. You leave us with little alternative but to take your life from you in return. However, we will listen to what you have to say. Do you wish to say anything?"

Frank could be seen mumbling something. George said, "I'm sorry, I didn't hear what you said. Please speak up."

Frank stood a little straighter and clearly said, "I don't want to die." Then he hung his head in shame.

"I suppose not," said George, "but as I have said, you leave us with little choice. We've been told you have been very contrite and have confessed your sins to God and prepared yourself for your punishment. We feel that perhaps we can offer you two other solutions. Number one, our doctor here says he can and is prepared to give you a frontal lobotomy. That would mean that you would be allowed to live a kind of life. You would have no thoughts whatsoever and would just sit around doing nothing. The other choice is complete castration. In this case you would become much less aggressive, as well as sexually repressed. If, however, for some reason it did not work and your aggressive nature persisted, then execution would be carried out immediately. What do you wish for your punishment to be, Mr. Howard?"

"I think my punishment should be castration," said Frank. "I feel I can be a better person and an asset to the community if given the opportunity."

"Your feelings and observations on this matter are appreciated, but our decision has not been influenced by your feelings. You will be operated on by the doctor in three days or less. After the operation you will be under round-the-clock guard for six months. After six months, the guard will be relaxed somewhat but you will be observed closely for the rest of your life. If you do not behave, you will be given a lethal injection. No reprieve will be given a second time."

The judges got up and left.

EPILOGUE

It's hard to believe that we've been here on Two Moons for three years now. Good old Earth is starting to fade from memory. I'm not sure whether that's a good thing or a bad thing. Today, we are hosting our anniversary celebration. Everyone has gathered in town for the big party. All the people working at our mines are here, as are the exploration teams. The celebration is set to last three days.

Nearly all the people living here now have their own brick home. George, Richard and I are living together. We all love the great outdoors, so we still camp out in our canvas-covered lean-to from time to time. The weather has stayed mild for the three years we've been here, so camping is possible year-round.

Many of the young families have grown and there are lots of new toddlers around. A couple of the folks who were single when they first arrived have since been married by Reverend Stead. And it appears that we might have another wedding to look forward to soon: Jimmy Richardson and Sheila Gransden have been spending an awful lot of time together. Reverend Stead's congregation had increased. Most people here believe in God—more now than prior to the meteor.

The livestock judging was already underway when George, Robert and I arrived. One of the Quonset huts had been set aside for livestock. Nearly every farm had a variety now. Most of the farms started off with a specialty stock, but they were well mixed now. All the farmers were very proud of what they had.

The main craft hall was in our hangar. It was badly damaged when the meteor hit but had since been fully restored. Our aircraft were all outside, polished up and on display for the crowd to look through. We had some student pilots on hand to explain things. The two 150 Cessnas were going to be flying most of the day, carrying those who wanted a ride. The flights were pretty short at about half an hour each. They were taking their passengers over the farms and the lake, as well as the town.

Nearly all of our womenfolk and some of the men had crafts and handiwork on display. These would be judged and ribbons would be handed out for prizes on Saturday afternoon. We had several displays of old skills like spinning and weaving set up, as well. It would take a good day just to get around to see everything.

We hadn't seen very much of the craft hall before George wanted to go on to see the livestock. He was particularly interested in the horses being shown.

"See that young filly there," said George excitedly. "She's mine. My mare couldn't win next Tuesday's race if she started now. She could never run a lick, but this beauty will."

"She does fill the eye," said Richard patiently. He had heard George excitedly extol the yearling's virtues previously. "She will certainly win the Best Young Filly ribbon."

"When she gets to the track, she'll be a winner there, as well," enthused George. "Look at those muscles already."

I wished him well and moved over to talk to Albert. He and Bonnie had a new colt they were justly proud of. Several other people had bought into the racing business. There was an air of excitement that just the mention of the races for the next two days would bring bubbling out of everyone. The anniversary had been declared as the date that all horses aged a year, no matter when they had been born. This was carrying on the age-old tradition.

Going outside for a breather, I spotted my grandson, Barry, Malcolm's son, as he drove by with a wagon filled with hay and a load of young kids. I didn't even know he knew how to drive a team of horses. I'd bet his dad couldn't drive horses; he never had been interested in things of that nature. My other three grandchildren were girls and interested in academics. Mathematics, stars, and business were their varied interests. Certainly not outdoor activities. I was glad Barry was interested, at least. I liked to think that one of my progeny shared my passions.

The children in the wagon seemed to be having a great time. Most of them were so young, they'd probably never been on a hayride before. Two boys' teams made up of five- to nine-year-olds were playing a game of soccer in our field inside the oval of the track. We had a baseball diamond now, as well as a soccer field. I could hear the parents cheering. It looked like everyone was having a good time. That's what it's all about, isn't it?

The Gransdens took a short turn on the stage after the soccer game had finished. It was already early afternoon. Where had the morning gone? The main thing was that everybody was enjoying the occasion. Everyone deserved this. Three years of hard work had paid off. Sheila Gransden had taught Jimmy to play the fiddle and guitar. He was taking his turn performing with the family. They sang many old favourites and the crowd was appreciative. When they were done, a pair of girls' soccer teams took to the field.

I wandered over to one of the refreshments stands. There were hot dogs that were not quite hot dogs. They tasted more like sausages on a bun. The hamburgers were quite like what I was used to, so I had one of those with a fruit drink. The fruit drinks were many and varied. The whole atmosphere was very pleasing and very much like a carnival. Mike came over to sit at the picnic bench I was occupying.

"I'm most proud of our mill at the falls," I said. "Three stories for the building is a bonus. We're able to have many industries all in the one place. You and Max did a super job getting all the bricks and cement together for it."

"Now that most of the houses and other needs are taken care of, I'll be cutting back on making large quantities. Max is bowing out of the business completely," said Mike.

"Did you know that we'll be supplying most of our power from there soon?"

"I heard the geologists had found copper a while back," Mike said, "congratulations."

"What are your plans for the future?" I asked. "Do you have another project in mind?"

"I feel I've worked very hard since coming here," said Mike. "Then again, everybody has. I might set up a small farm and get your friends to show me what to do on it. Or, I suppose I could always take up fishing."

Robert sat down with us. "Where's George?" I asked. "Still admiring his horses?"

"Yep, he's still at it." Robert said. "He needs something else to do. Can't you find some task that will take up some of his time?"

"I saw you at the Gransdens' performance sitting with Sue," I said. "What's the latest word there?"

"We're good friends. We just like to do things together sometimes," he replied. "For instance, we're going to the dance tonight."

"That should be a lot of fun—everybody is looking forward to it," I answered.

The amateur actors took to the stage as the second soccer game ended. They put on a nice little comedy play that was enjoyed by the crowd. The people were in a good mood to start with and an easy-going comedy was the best possible topper. Many of the children were too excited to eat, but there was plenty of food on hand for those who weren't.

A teen baseball game was next on the agenda for the sports area. It was mixed girls and boys. It was a good game to watch. The young people were very skilled, and the score stayed close all the way through the game. The teams were well matched. The shepherds were demonstrating sheep herding just to the north of the track. It was well worth watching, and while the young dogs were a little too eager at times, they all knew what was required of them and put on a good show.

I went down to the craft hall and spent another leisurely hour looking at all the things there. I had tasted Marie's preserves before, but she had a few combinations I had never tried. All of them were delicious. No wonder she had volunteered to look after the fruit.

For supper, several pigs had been barbecued whole. It had been a good first day of festivities. Now for the dancing. I had never seen such a crowd at a barn dance before. A crowded barn I had seen, but this was everybody on the planet, including kids, from infants on up. All the existing picnic tables from across Two Moons had been brought over to provide seating, and still many people were seated on the grass. Robert and George had acquired a table but the table was shared with Dan and Betty, as well as Marie and all the kids. Jimmy was the only one missing and he was up on the platform with the rest of the musicians.

I just wanted to be a spectator, but I had many ladies making sure I got my exercise. Marie was the first to get me up for a little do-si-do, followed closely by nearly every woman I knew. I had a great time but was worn out far too soon. The younger kids just crashed and slept were they fell. Moms and dads were busy carrying them back to the family campsite. The general opinion was that all the children had a day like no other.

I slept so soundly George had to shake me awake next morning. I ached in places I didn't even know existed. Thankfully, there were only two more days of celebrating to go. I would stay away from dancing if I could help it.

The next two days were very similar to the first. The celebration was the climax of three years of hard work. Everybody was blowing off steam. We had accomplished a lot of progress.

The future is looking bright. I'm very proud of my grandchildren; they are bright and active, but I guess all grandparents feel that way. My wife, had she lived, would certainly be proud, as well.